MIDNIGHT STAR

MIDNIGHT STAR

Karpov Kinrade

DARING
BOOKS

KarpovKinrade.com
Copyright © 2016 Karpov Kinrade
Cover Art Copyright © 2016 Karpov Kinrade

~~~~~

Published by Daring Books

~~~~~

First Edition

~~~~~

ISBN-10: 1939559448
ISBN-13: 9781939559449

Disclaimer

This is a work of fiction. Names, characters, places and inci-
dents are products of the author's imagination, or the author
has used them fictitiously.

Dedicated to Ed, Carol, and Steve
Salt (of) the earth
Not all battles can be won with swords
Some are won with words

TABLE OF CONTENTS

NOTE FROM THE AUTHOR

This is *Midnight Star,* book 2 in the *Vampire Girl* series. For your enjoyment, we highly recommend you read the books in order. Book 1, *Vampire Girl*, can be found wherever books are sold. Happy reading!

1

DEAD KING

"Our father, King Lucian. He could be... difficult, at times, but he was always fair."

—Asher

Lesson number one in making a deal with the devil... never trust the devil. Asher charmed me. He made me believe his lies. And now he stands here before me, with his infuriating smirk and a mouth full of deceit, expecting me to trust him. Again.

Fool me once, shame on you. Fool me twice. Just, no.

"Ari, please allow me to explain," he says, his words like soft caresses.

I am not swayed. "I can't believe anything you say, so why should I listen?" I cross my arms over my chest, hiding the fresh blood from the wrist wound I reopened against the stone edge of the table. I try to keep from trembling, and I try to hide the demon mark I drew in blood on the wall behind me. Fen is summoned. He will come. Now, I can only hope I live long enough to see him. I sneeze, and groan with the realization that being stuck in a frozen cave with a sick vampire gave me the flu. My head is heavy and my skin is hot. Still, I must keep my wits about me.

The walls are dark and rough, dimly lit by torches casting blue light, flickering sinister shadows on the cold bare floor. In places, white crystal erupts from the stone, as if threatening to consume the entire room.

Asher steps closer. "I can understand why you distrust me, but I promise, it's not what you think."

His father, King Lucian, who was supposed to be dead, sits quietly, drinking from a silver goblet. Grey lines streak his black hair. A red cape falls from his shoulders. Black armor clads his body. The king studies me like men study horses, his dark blue eyes cold and calculating. His lips betray no emotion. He lets his son do all the talking.

"So you didn't lie to your brothers?" I ask. "Didn't hide the fact the king still lives, or let Fen investigate a murder that never happened? You didn't conspire to kidnap me and bring me here?" There's a tone to my voice my mother would have called snarky. And it's the thought of her that sends chills up my back. "What will happen to my mother?" I yell loudly, harshly, as spit flies from my mouth. I can no longer fulfill my bargain of spending time with each prince. I can no longer choose one to marry.

Asher doesn't respond.

I ask again, slower, my eyes drilling into his. "What. Happens. To. My. Mother?"

He holds up his hand and takes a step toward me. He has his father's blue eyes, his black hair. "She will be safe. I give you my word."

I laugh. "As if your word means anything right now."

"Ari, please—"

"How could you do this?" I hiss at him. "Fen trusted you above all. And you betrayed him. You betrayed *me*."

Asher sighs. His hand falls to his side. The playfulness is gone from his face, replaced by something darker. "Things aren't always black and white. Not in your world, and certainly not in mine. My brothers want war. They want to enslave the Fae. *Your* people. Is that what you want?"

I pause, struck by his words. I haven't even had time to consider the implications of what they've told me. I'm Fae? How?

Asher takes another step forward, and I adjust, keeping my body between him and the demon mark. I need to—

"Move out of the way, girl," Lucian says.

I don't obey.

The king stands. When he walks toward me, I can almost feel the room shake from his heavy iron boots. He draws a sword from his side, giant and grey. A horned skull of some beast makes the guard of the blade, and foreign symbols engrave the steel. The king lifts the sword one-handed and points it at my neck. It must be three times the size of Spero. How can this man lift it? And then I remember... this is no man. This is the monster who drove the Fae from their world and enslaved their race. This is the monster who claimed my mother's soul.

"Move," the king commands.

I shuffle to the side, and the sword presses against my throat, drawing a speck of blood.

Asher's eyes land on the mark. He looks to me, sadness on his face. He says nothing.

For the first time, Lucian's lips show emotion, curling into a grimace. "You summoned the Prince of War? Do you have any idea what he would do to this kingdom, these people, if he finds a way here?"

I don't respond. He will have no pity from me.

"Asher, take this... *Princess*... to her quarters. Until she knows the truth, she must be kept under guard."

I ball my fists, my knuckles turning white. "You will not keep me here. You—

He whips his blade forward. The blunt side hits my ribs, throwing me back. I crash into the wall, the air leaving my lungs in a rush.

"You are a dog," Lucian spits. "A dog. And you will know your place at your master's heel." He turns away, whispers something to Asher, and leaves.

The Prince of Pride reaches for me.

I pull back, cradling my sore ribs, rolling up into a ball. Tears sting my eyes from the pain.

"I am sorry, Arianna."

I spit at him.

He doesn't recoil. He doesn't even seem shocked. "Madrid and Durk will take you to your room. They will take care of you." He walks out, following his father.

The woman and one of the men—the short one—who helped kidnap me approach. Durk throws a bag over my head and ties it at the throat, making it hard to breathe. Madrid secures my wrists behind my back. They push me forward, and I nearly trip over my own feet as they roughly guide me through a door and down corridors I can't see.

I hear yelling. Asher. "I can handle the Princess."

Lucian. "You have grown too soft. Too fond of the girl."

"I have grown compassionate. Isn't that why we fight?"

"We fight for many reasons. We need the Midnight Star, but we must stay in command. We must—"

I am thrown into a room. The door locks behind me. Madrid loosens her iron grip and leans in to speak quietly in my ear. "I apologize for this treatment, Your Grace. Soon, all shall be revealed, and you will understand how important you are to your people."

"My parents were human," I say through the bag. "I'm human. You have the wrong girl."

Durk laughs, but it's Madrid who speaks. "You are half human, which is a problem for some. For those who believe the throne should only be inhabited by the purest of our kind. But your blood is the most powerful, that of the High Fae, that of the royal line. You are heir to our lands, heir to Avakiri. And everyone shall soon see that your human half has not corrupted what you are. You will wake the ancient powers of our kind and bring balance back to the Four Tribes. And then we will free our people and rule our world once again."

Her words are heavy with the promise of war, of bloodshed, of death. And I know whose death she calls for. The vampires. The demons. Maybe even the Shade. Anyone who shares the blood of their oppressors.

My friends. The people I have grown to love.

My mind pulls back to her other words. "Half human?" I know my mother is human. Isn't she? But then, I thought I was human too. What of my father?

Click. Another door unlocks, and I'm escorted through it. Madrid gently sits me down into a chair. She pulls the bag off my head, and I blink a few times to acclimate my eyes to light again. How could this be? This is no dungeon. No medieval torture chamber. I'm in a spacious bedroom suite complete with a blazing fire and plush four-poster bed. I sit at a small table with two chairs, and I study the light oak bookshelf, desk, dresser, armoire, and door, which presumably leads to a bathroom. The king treats me like a slave, and yet I am given the rooms of a princess.

My hands are still tied together. I check the window. Bars over it from the outside. So, it is a cage, a gilded one, but a cage nonetheless.

Undoubtedly, the door to my room will be locked from without.

Madrid leans over to untie my hands. White furs cover her body, and brown leather covers her legs. A red cord is tied around her waist.

Durk grumbles. A brown bear pelt spills over his shoulder. "Should keep her locked up. No telling what she'll do."

Madrid clucks at him. "She's already done the worst, summoning the Prince of War. She doesn't have her powers yet. She's harmless. And we need her to cooperate."

"We only need her blood to cooperate," he says.

7

Madrid ignores him and takes the chair opposite me, forcing Durk to remain standing. Her white hair is long, nearly touching the floor, flowing down her back in several braids. "Haven't you figured it out yet?" she asks.

I shake my head, because though pieces are clicking together, the picture they make is too confusing for my pounding head to make sense of.

"Your father was High Fae. He was in line to be king. This was thousands of years ago, of course. Back when there were any royalty of our kind left. Back before the princes and their demon spawn destroyed everything, killing into near extinction our very race, wiping out the royal line entirely."

"Except my father," I say, my throat dry.

"Except your father," she says. "He had already been banished from this kingdom and sent to your world as punishment, to live amongst humans, forever hiding who he was. He was meant to live in the shadows, to scrape by in obscurity for what he did. But it seems he couldn't behave, even there. He fell in love. With a human. He tarnished his bloodline and created a child who was half human. And then he got himself killed, and you and your mother disappeared. Until now."

"My father was Fae? Royalty?" My fever is spiking. Everything feels disjointed. Unreal. I shiver, but I am so hot I want to peel my own skin off.

Madrid responds, but her words blur together, like two composers playing different songs at the same time.

My eyes close, and the world turns upside down. Something hard hits my head. Someone yells. Hands on my body. Cold. So cold on my hot skin.

I'm being lifted and carried and I don't care because all I want to do is follow the darkness into nothingness.

And so I do.

...

When I wake, I'm wrapped in layers of blankets and wearing a long cotton gown. My hair is a nest of tangles spread over my pillow, and my head still aches, but at least I'm not hallucinating. I try to sit up, but a voice stops me. "Take it slow. You're still weak."

Madrid comes into my view, her flawlessly youthful face juxtaposed against her long white hair and ancient eyes. Her pointed ears are tipped with silver earrings shaped like waves, and she wears a long sea foam green gown pulled at the waist with a thin silver tie. Silver and blue designs cover the hem and chest, and a blue cape falls over her shoulder.

"How long have I been here?" I ask.

"You slept through the night and most of the day. I gave you medicine to heal your illness. Still, you'll feel

9

tired for a few days." She slips a hand behind my back and helps me sit up. The room is warm, the fireplace blazing. I've soaked through my clothing and sheets, and my skin feels clammy, but not nearly as hot as before. "My fever broke," I say.

Madrid nods. "I should have seen how sick you were, but there were other matters to focus on. It was careless of me. You're too valuable to lose."

I look around to make sure the creepy man isn't around before I ask my next question. "Durk said you just needed my blood. Why?"

She hands me a cup of water and sits on a chair by my bed as I drink greedily. I didn't realize how thirsty I am.

"The magic of our people is dying," she says. "When the demons came from the sky and slaughtered the High Fae, the Spirits left us."

"Spirits?"

"There are five, and they go by many names. We call them Riku, Wadu, Tauren, Zyra, and Yami. Riku is fire, passion, and the shaping of truth. Wadu is water, peace, and healing. Tauren is earth, strength, and life. Zyra is wind, knowledge, and wisdom. And Yami... Yami is all of them, and none of them. Yami is life. Death. Balance. Hope. He has more names than the others. One you may have heard... the Midnight Star."

She stares into the fireplace, her eyes distant, lost in some faraway memory. "When the last High Fae died, Yami died with her. Our magic began to fade. The other Spirits grew weak and turned to slumber. They were locked away, hidden throughout our world, to be kept safe for when…" She stares into my eyes. "For when Midnight Star returns."

I swallow the lump in my throat. "I can't help you."

"You can. You will." She grabs my hand. "If your blood is strong enough, and I believe it is, you can reverse our plight. You can bring back the ancient ones and restore our magic. Only then can we survive. Only then can we *live*."

I pull my hand away. "I'm the wrong girl. Find someone else."

She smiles, and it's a sad, wistful smile. "There is no one else. We Fae are bound to our magic. And when our magic dies, we die."

I say nothing. I can't tell her what she wants to hear.

Madrid sighs. She opens her mouth, as if to say something, but then she stands and heads to the door. "I'll leave you to bathe and dress. Now that you're awake, we mustn't lose any time."

Before she leaves, I have one more question. "Did you know my father?"

She pauses. "Yes, I knew him well. You have his eyes."

"What was he like?"

11

She cocks her head, thinking. "He was impetuous. Reckless. Careless. But he was also kind. He was a good man who didn't deserve his fate." With those words, she closes the door, and I hear the lock click.

I carefully lift my body out of bed, testing my own weight on my shaking legs. The cold stone floor is covered in carpets that cushion my steps and keep my feet warm. I walk slowly to the door I assume is the bathroom and find a large tub in the center filled with steaming water. There is a robe draped over a chair by the bath, and jars of scented oils and soaps sit on the ledge. I step in, testing the heat with my toe, then pull off my gown and sink into the hot water.

My body is full of bruises and aches, and the heat steals some of them away, at least for a time. I sniff at the bottles of soaps and pick one that smells of roses to drop into my bath.

Then I lean back and close my eyes. I wish I could escape for a moment. Pretend I am home with Fen, with Baron waiting for me on my bed. Or more likely sitting by the bath with his head leaning on the tub's ledge for me to pet.

Home. Is that what Stonehill is to me now? Home? Not Oregon? Not my mother? But Stonehill Castle and Fen and Baron and Kayla and...

Daison.

Daison is dead.

How could I have forgotten? How could his death have been locked so deeply into my mind that I'm just now remembering? Does Kayla know? Have they found his body? Do they even know where to look?

The Fae. Their attack killed him. He was Fae. He was one of them. Shade or not, he was Fae too. And they think I will help them? That I will forgive and forget what they've done to my friends?

But Fen has Shade slaves. Fen is part of the system that destroyed and killed Fae and took over their world. Fen must have known who I was and he didn't tell me. Fen lied to me just like everyone else.

If I was Fae, I might want all the vampires dead too.

If I was Fae, I would want to free my people.

And I am Fae, I realize. It's still such an odd thought. I'm Fae. And I do want the Fae and the Shade freed.

But I don't want to kill the vampires. I don't want to help people who think it's okay to kill the innocent.

I sink down, submerging my head. Underwater, the sounds of the world disappear. Only the thrum of the water itself fills me. I hold my breath as long as I can and squeeze my eyes shut, trying to empty my mind of everything but the moment.

When I rise to the surface and suck in air, I am no closer to any answers. I don't know what is right and what is wrong. I don't know who is lying to me and who is telling me the truth.

If there's anything I've learned in life, it's that reality is never black and white. And I have to muck through a lot of ambiguous grey to figure out where I stand.

I sigh and climb out of the tub, the water and bubbles dripping off my body. I shiver, already missing the warmth, but I'm not going to get any answers here.

Once I'm dry, I search my room for suitable clothing. How many times can a girl find herself in a strange castle stocked with strange clothing that happens to fit? Too many times, apparently.

I don't find any badass leather pants and tunic that Fen would grin at.

I find plenty of outfits Asher would like, which makes me extra grumpy. Reluctantly, I slip on an ankle-length black dress with long flared sleeves and a silver tie that wraps around my waist. Like Madrid's dress, this one has silver embroidery at the hem and neckline and features a cape sewn into the back. I can't place the fabric. It's soft, silky, but more durable than silk or satin. I must admit it's comfortable.

I find a pair of shoes, something less functional than my boots but more functional than heels, and slip them on. There's a mirror here. I haven't seen a proper mirror in a long time, not since I entered Hell. It's strange seeing my reflection so clearly, rather than catching glimpses in water or reflective cutlery. It's not a great ego boost. I'm too pale with dark circles under my eyes, and my hair is a tangled mess even after my bath. I dig through the dresser to find a brush, then do my best to tame my hair until it falls over my shoulders. Nothing can be done about my complexion except some sun and time, so I give up on that and check the door in my room. Locked.

I expected that, but still... even the princes of hell—demons of legend—didn't keep me locked up like a prisoner. This is how the people who think I'm their long lost Fae Princess treat me? I'm not impressed.

I check the window, pulling on the black bars that block my escape. Too hard. My hands ache. And if I did get out, where would I go? Could I find my way back to the elevator?

I sit down on the bed, planning out my next move. When Madrid returns, perhaps I can push past her and escape. Maybe I can—

The door opens, and it's not Madrid. It's Asher, looking contrite and entirely too apologetic. He brought food. With chocolate.

How devious.

He hands me the platter, and the smell makes my stomach rumble. Sautéed vegetables, fresh green salad, warm bread with honey butter, fresh berries with cream, and a slice of rich chocolate cake drizzled with a white cream sauce. I scowl at him, but take my food to the table and sit. I must eat to regain my strength.

"No meat?" I ask, needing more energy before I dive into the hard questions.

He shakes his head. "Only the Fire Tribe eats meat. It's frowned upon by the other Tribes."

I nod and dig in, savoring each bite. Asher wisely stays silent until I've licked my fingers clean, and I sit back in my chair, my belly full and my mood much improved by the sustenance. "You faked your father's death." It's not a question, because in this I feel certain.

Asher laughs. "I wondered if he had told you... no..." he mumbles, speaking half to himself. "No... I suppose he didn't trust either of us." The Prince of Pride stares back at me, his voice clear and cold. "Fen poisoned our father."

I tremble. "Another lie."

He leans forward, smiling. "Oh no, dear Princess. This, I assure you, is true. Our father told Fen of his plans to free the slaves. In return, your precious demon poisoned his own flesh and blood. I don't believe he planned to kill our father, only lock him up, interrogate him, possibly overthrow him altogether."

"But he didn't," I say, looking for holes in his lie.

"He never got the chance. You see, father told me he has always been cautious with poisons. He has built a resistance to many of them. After Fen completed his dirty deed, he left father alone, likely to fetch chains. But it only took a moment for Lucian to reawaken. He realized what happened. His own son had betrayed him. Fen, the kind, honorable one. How would Levi or Dean react? Niam? No. He knew then he could never free the slaves as King of the Vampires. He had to leave, go into hiding. He had to join with the Fae. So my father took one of his own concoctions, one he had used during the invasion, one that feigns death."

"But I saw his body—"

"You saw the remains of a dead vampire Lucian placed in his grave after his potion wore off and he left the mausoleum."

His story makes sense, except Fen is no poisoner. "How do you know all this?"

"Because Lucian told me. He needed someone still on the inside. So, he came to me, said I was the last one he could trust."

Images flash through my mind. Fen glaring at Asher. Fen upset Lucian always trusted Asher more. Did he... did he really poison his father?

Asher raises an eyebrow, seeing the uncertainty in my face. He holds a silver goblet to his lips, drinking. "I want peace, Ari. I want the Fae and vampire and Shade to live side-by-side without war, without slavery, without hate. Yes, I knew you were a Fae Princess, but I never lied to you. I never told you anything that wasn't true. My father's will *did* demand your commitment to marry one of us. It came into effect when he resigned his crown, even though my brothers thought him dead. He knew he couldn't make a deal with you himself, not while in hiding. He knew he needed you in this world. Your mother set this up sixteen years ago when you died, and she sold her soul to bring you back to life. My father took the deal and waited. We couldn't force you here. You had to come willingly."

He takes a deep breath and closes his eyes for a long moment before opening them again. He speaks softly, without the typical arrogance I'm used to. "You're the only hope this world has of surviving."

I shake my head, stunned by his calm demeanor. "So this is all justified in your mind? You just did as you had to?"

"Yes. Maybe there was a better way, but I don't know what that would have been. Ari, I'm begging you, please believe me. I'm not your enemy. I care about you."

He reaches for my hand and I don't pull away. My mind is filled with too many conflicting emotions.

"I won't lie," he says. "I want to be king. Out of all my brothers, I think I would be the best choice. Out of all of us, I alone want peace. I alone want to end this war. And with you, I know I can."

His eyes fill with sorrow and something else... hope. "Give me this month, Ari. Your mother will be kept safe. The contract will not be broken. You will visit your world. You will fulfill your obligation by spending time with me. Give me this month to prove I'm the best choice for this world. Give me this month to win back your trust."

I suck in my breath, then pull away my hand slowly. "Do you know what Fen told me after I found out who he really was?"

Asher shakes his head.

"He said not to trust anyone, least of all him or his brothers."

2

LIKE RAPUNZEL

"My brothers and I have been around a very long time.
You couldn't even fathom how long if you tried."

—Fenris Vane

My last words silence Asher. He sits across from me, waiting for me to speak, to make some kind of decision about what I will do. I'm not in a position to escape at the moment—in my barred prison cell, so I must make do until an opportunity presents itself. If that means I must play this game for now... I will.

"I don't know what to believe, Asher. But if you swear to me this will continue to fulfill my contract, that my mother will be safe, I will spend time with you. I can't promise it will sway me to do what you want. But I won't spit in your face again... unless you really deserve it."

He chuckles, standing as well. "Fair enough, Princess. Fair enough. I swear your mother will be safe, the contract fulfilled."

I cock my head at him, a hint of a smile on my lips. "Wasn't Dean supposed to have his turn with me? He won't like this."

Asher smiles, displaying adorable dimples. "It's good for him to have his desires thwarted once in a while." He holds out his arm. "Would you like to see more of your current home? I believe you have a destiny to fulfill and Madrid and Durk are waiting."

I take his arm but crinkle my nose. "I don't like Durk."

Asher smirks. "No one likes Durk. Durk doesn't even like Durk. Just ignore him."

I nod as we walk out of the bedroom and into one of the most magnificent hallways I've ever seen. A crystal chandelier shines from the ceiling. Purple rugs cover the floor. I place my hand on the black marble wall erupting with clear gemstone. "What is this place?"

"It is what remains of the Crystal Palace. It was built inside a mountain," Asher says.

We walk through the stone hallway, into a passage built from glass. Small waterfalls fall behind the clear walls. At the end of the hallway Madrid and Durk meet us.

"I was just telling Ari about the palace," Asher says. "But you know more about it than I."

Madrid nods and leads us past giant doors, outside the palace, and into the huge cave I glimpsed before. All around us, Fae go about their business. One man, giant and coiled with muscle, works at a forge, crafting a sword. It makes me miss my own sword, Spero. I'll have to find a way to get it back.

Another Fae, small and with long blue hair, tends to wounded men and women lying in cots along the side of the cave wall. "What happened to them?" I ask.

"They were injured fighting the vampires," Madrid says.

So they're the Raiders. They don't just keep to the Outlands like Fen thinks.

"This is our capital, where the High Fae once ruled," Madrid explains. "It has since fallen into disarray. Into chaos and ruin."

Durk snorts. "It's turned into a shithole, is what she means."

We walk deeper through the caves, and I see the truth in their words. A hopelessness clings to the people here. The shiny wonder of the crystal looses its luster when you look closer and see the dirt and cracks. Before us, a chunk of crystal rests on its side, the ruined top of a palace tower. Few Fae occupy this area, and no children. They are the homeless, the vagabonds, the nameless... the broken. This is no city, but a carcass slowly rotting. Once it would have been magnificent. I glimpse the beauty in its shadows. In its memories. But now it is nothing but food for the crows.

We exit the caves and climb a long staircase with clear walls. Through them, I see the palace carved into the mountain like an old sculpture worn away by time. "This is where my father lived, isn't it?"

Madrid nods. "Not only him, but your entire family once called this home."

I turn to Asher, frowning, as the bigger story takes shape in my mind. "And you killed them. You and your kind, you wiped out the Fae, the royal family."

Asher turns his head, a look of shame on his face. "That was a long time ago."

"I don't understand," I tell him. "You speak of peace, but you almost destroyed an entire race... What makes you different now?"

Asher's jaw hardens, and he turns to me, his voice resolute. "I never... I never wanted war. But I didn't do enough to stop it. I failed." His hand balls into a fist. "I won't fail again."

Wait... He didn't want the war?

I sigh. There's still so much I don't know about Asher, Fen, their history. This world. I want to ask more questions, but we step through a door at the end of the staircase, and the cold wind strikes my face.

We are outside, near the top of the snow-peaked mountain. Lands of green and blue spread before us.

I shiver, trying to stay warm as my eyes adjust to the brightness.

Asher wraps his cloak around me.

I don't want his help, but... it is a warm cloak. "Thanks."

He smiles. "See, we're getting along already."

I shake my head. He's still my captor. We are *not* getting along.

"Keep up," yells Durk. He and Madrid lead us up a winding stone staircase carved into the side of the mountain.

"Where are we going?" My voice is nearly lost on the wind.

Asher points, and I look up. Three great beasts fly toward the top of the mountain. They each have the body, tail and back legs of a lion, and the head, wings and talons of an eagle. One is covered in white feathers, its paws and fur gold. The other is black and red, and the third is silver. I gasp. "Are those... "

"Gryphon," Asher says. "We must travel to the Air Realm, and this is the only way."

I gulp as we reach the summit of the mountain. "We're going to ride them?"

King Lucian waits for us at the peak, and when he sees me, he climbs atop the black gryphon, pulling on the reins of the wild beast clawing into the snow. Madrid and Durk climb atop the silver gryphon, whispering to each other. Asher guides me to white and gold one, holding out his hand. "After you, Princess."

The beast is huge, magnificent, and entirely intimidating. Each of its claws are the size of my hands. The saddle is giant and embellished with gold. If I was scared to ride a horse, I can hardly register what I'm feeling right now.

Asher leans in, his hand on my waist. "I won't let anything happen to you. This is entirely safe," he says against my ear. "Well… usually."

His teasing only gives me more resolve. I straighten my back, square my shoulders and mount the gryphon. Asher follows suit, wrapping his arms around me and pressing his body against mine. "At last," he says, "I get you all to myself."

I can't help but laugh. His flirtations feel so artificial, but his affection is genuine and so harmless, fun… innocent. I don't know how I know this, but I do.

I lean over the beast's neck and pat its head. "Hey there, buddy. I don't know how to do this, but I just want to thank you for taking us where we need to go. Please don't drop me, and I'll do my best to ride you gently."

I turn to Asher. "So how do you control one of these—"

Asher pulls on the reins, and the gryphon leaps off the mountain and into the air.

I scream.

I feel like I'm about to die.

And then—*then* I feel more alive than I've ever been.

I'm flying.

On a creature that shouldn't even exist.

It's a cool day, and the air hits my face hard, and I breathe it in deeply and smile, holding on to a leather strap that's harnessed around the gryphon.

We fly higher and higher, and I let out a call of sheer joy as we soar into the sky, white clouds swirling around us. I no longer feel the pressure of Asher at my back, or the heavy stares of Durk and Madrid flying next to us. I no longer fear the long fall below me, or the weight of the choices weighing on my soul. I just feel free. Happy. Alive. Airborne!

But as the Crystal Palace fades from my view, worry sets in. I called Fen with his blood mark at the palace, but if he comes for me, I will no longer be there. I must find a way to call him again, once I get where I am going.

I note any land marks below us, in case I need to find my way back: a giant brown tree cascading over a forest, a long gleaming river.

I don't know how long the flight lasts, but soon I see a floating island in the sky, surrounded by clouds that look more corporeal than I know them to be. The gryphon land on the edge of the island, in a clearing surrounded by silver trees. Above, on ragged cliffs, other gryphon roar. They have chains around their paws, tying them to the mountain.

"This must be like a Fae airport," I say to Asher. "Gryphon International, maybe?"

He just rolls his eyes. Silly vampire. No sense of humor.

As Asher and I slide off the gryphon—me with as much grace as I can muster—a group of Fae dressed in white and blue robes approach us. The man leading them has long white hair and a very long white beard pulled into three braids with feathers woven into them. He scowls at us. "Madrid, Durk, you are not wanted here. And how dare you bring these... " he sneers, waving his hand at Asher and Lucian... "these creatures to our Tribe."

"They are on our side, Norin," Madrid explains patiently. "They found her." She pulls me forward. "The Midnight Star."

The group of Fae behind Norin come alive in hushed whispers, staring at me, but the man stays quiet, glancing my way for the briefest of assessment. "The last High Fae? She looks too human to be of any use. But we shall see." He looks back at Madrid. "You may stay three days. If she can summon the Midnight Star, we shall reassess."

"Dana and Dala will show you to your quarters," he says, gesturing to the two women at his side. They are twins, identical in every way, from their long sapphire hair to their matching robes. "Be advised, we are a peaceful tribe. There will be no violence of any kind tolerated here." He glares at the vampires. "We wish no part in this war you have thrust upon us."

"We understand," Madrid says, bowing. "You will not have any trouble from us." She gives warning looks to Lucian and Asher, and I suppress a grin. I'm not sure the vampires are the problem in this scenario. They have brought me here against my will. It's the human girl they should be worried about.

Dana and Dala—who I can't tell apart at all because they sound and speak the same—escort us through the city. A gentle breeze blows through the streets, carrying the smell of exotic flowers. We travel through the town center, where the streets are full of Fae going about their daily lives. Children play some kind of air ball game in a small park between shops, while their parents browse the local wares. The path we walk is lined with tall trees decorated with bells and chimes that catch the wind, creating a song around us. Long banners of white and blue fall from two towers in the center of town. The spires are works of art, carved from stone and glass and glinting in the sun. There are holes carved into them, reminding me of abstract paintings, and I wonder how they manage to stand.

"Those are the main libraries," Dana, or Dala, says. "We are renowned for our thirst and love of knowledge. We collect the histories of our people, stories and tales. We study them."

The other twin speaks. "The Air Tribe produces the scholars of the Fae, the teachers and historians and storytellers."

We reach a tall tree with a staircase carved into the center and glass hallways branching off from the trunk. The twins lead us up the stairs and turn down one glass hallway toward a large bedroom.

It's made of wood and grey stone, with windows that take up most of three walls. Except they are not covered by glass, but by sheer white drapes that sway in the sweet-smelling wind.

You wouldn't want to be afraid of heights in this bedroom. A fall off the outdoor balconies would end in death or serious breakage of body parts.

My bed is situated in the middle of the room, a four-poster canopy bed with more sheer white drapes hanging from the carved wooden frame. They rise like tree vines from the floor and almost reach the tall vaulted ceilings.

Asher escorts me in. "I'll come by tomorrow. Be well, Princess. There will be guards at your door through the night to make sure you are safe."

Yeah right. More like, to make sure I stay put.

The prince walks to the door, then turns to look at me. "I think we can be of help to one another, Arianna. I think we can be friends, even. There is hope for this, after all. *Dum spiro spero*."

He closes the door, and I wait for his footsteps to fade.

Alone in my room, I stand on the balcony of my bedroom, staring out at a picturesque vision of mountains and sky as far as the eye can see. No barred windows, but it's still a prison, nonetheless.

I feel like Rapunzel, trapped in a tower waiting for a prince to come save me. But the damsel in distress isn't a role I enjoy playing.

So I decide to take matters into my own hands. I'm not going to wait around for someone to save me. I'm going to save myself.

Time to think outside the box. Or rather, the gilded cage perched high in a tree.

I look over the balcony and estimate how much cloth I would need to climb to the ground. Then I pull drapes from the windows and tie them together. I may not have the hair of Rapunzel, but I'll make due.

Before I attempt this, I need a backup plan. I need a way for Fen to find me here, just in case. I search the room for something sharp. When I find nothing useful, I study the mirror above the vanity. That will work. I wrap some cloth around my elbow and use it break the mirror. I grab a piece of sharp glass. With it, I cut my finger and use the blood to draw Fen's demon mark on the floor.

Now I'm ready. I throw my long makeshift rope over the balcony and tie it to the bed. My heart pounds in my chest. My hands are sweaty. It's a long way down. But I can't sit here waiting for others to decide my fate.

The sun is setting, and I consider waiting until it's fully dark, but what if someone returns? I have no guarantee I'll be left alone for the night. I stand at the edge of my balcony, looking over the cliff my room is carved into. A forest of silver trees grows at the bottom. A long... long... way down.

Come on. You can do this.

I climb over the wooden railing of the balcony and use my hands and feet to move down the knotted cloth. I move slowly. I do not look at the ground. Breathe in. Breathe out. Focus. Relax. Just—

A gust of wind hits me, shoving me against the cliff. The stone scrapes my knees and elbows. The rope tears into my wrist, reopening my wound and coating the cloth in blood, making it slippery.

The wind passes. I grip harder and continue my descent. The grove of silver trees is close. As long as no one looks in my direction, I should make it okay.

Lower.

Lower.

I run out of cloth. The ground isn't too far away. I shouldn't break anything if I drop. I take a deep breath and let go, falling into a roll as I land, just like Fen taught me. A bit of air is knocked out of me, but nothing is broken, and I can still walk—mostly, so I call it a success. It takes a moment to situate myself and figure out which direction I need to go.

I hear someone above me, at my balcony, and I hide in the shadows, half running, half limping toward the mountains with the gryphon. The sun has set. The streets are nearly empty.

It doesn't take me long to find my way to Gryphon International. I need to fly back to the Crystal Palace, using the landmarks I remember, and take the elevator back to the Seven Realms.

I climb the stone steps and seek out the gold and white gryphon I rode earlier. It's resting like a cat against a tree. I move closer, cautiously approaching the magnificent beast. It notices me and jumps up on its back legs, roaring at me as it bears down its claws. I raise my arms in defense.

And the talons tear into my flesh.

It's a deep, burning wound across my forearm, and I bite my lip to avoid crying out from the pain.

The gryphon steps back, cautious of me. But at least he's not attacking anymore.

I hear yelling from behind me. Someone is coming. I have to act fast.

I step forward, my good hand outstretched, and make soothing sounds as I approach.

The gryphon allows me to draw near, and I pat its head. "Good boy. Can I ride you now? Would that be okay?" The gryphon seems to think about my request, then lowers to the floor, bowing his head. I pull off the shackle around his leg and climb onto the saddle more gracefully than before.

The yelling grows louder.

I grab the reins and tug, and the gryphon launches into the air.

We dive off the island, fast, the wind tearing at my wounds and the night freezing my bones. The ground comes closer and closer.

I tug on the reins. "Up!"

But my gryphon keeps flying straight down. We need to level out. I pull harder, and he surges up, pushing me back in the saddle so fast I lose my grip and fall to the side. My leg catches in a leather strap, and I flip upside down, dangling like a rag doll off the saddle. The gryphon lurches wildly in the sky, confused without his rider guiding him.

I reach for my leg, trying to pull myself up, but my one arm is nearly useless from the cuts and blood, and it's hard to find purchase. I catch my ankle and attempt to leverage myself into a better position, but my bloody hands slips. The leather strap breaks.

And I fall.

The earth rushes up to greet me, and I know in this moment I am going to die. I will be a splat of blood and bone on a world I don't understand.

I close my eyes. I don't want to see when death steals me. Instead, I think of my mother, how she sang to me when I was little. I think of Fen, how his arms felt around me, how tight he held me when he was sleeping.

And then I feel arms around me. Real flesh and blood arms.

I no longer fall. I float through the sky.

I peel my eyes open, his name on my lips. "Fen?"

Asher smiles down at me. "Not quite, love."

...

We fly higher until we land on a cliff far above Air Island. Asher carries me off the black gryphon he guided and sits me down against a silver tree. My arm burns with pain, blood dripping everywhere from my wrist and forearm.

He doesn't speak, just rips strips of cloth off his nice suit and wraps them around my cuts until they stop bleeding. When he's finished, he sits in front of me, his face hard. "You almost died!"

I rub my arm, flinching from the pain. "I'd rather die than be a prisoner."

He pauses, the anger draining from his eyes. He falls back to sit on a stone, the moon bright behind him. "I never wanted you to be a prisoner. I wanted to tell you the truth... have you join the Fae willingly. But my father, he doesn't trust you."

"You don't have to follow him," I say. "You are your own man."

Asher looks at me with more vulnerability than I've ever seen in him. "He's my father. He's the King. He's taught me all I know."

Despite my anger and pain, something in his eyes tugs at me. I put a hand on his. "You're the better man."

He snorts. "I've had millenniums of people telling me otherwise." Asher's eyes drift to the sky above us, a sky full of stars. "Sometimes... Sometimes I just wish for home."

"Your realm?"

"No." He shakes his head. "Home. My true home. Where my brothers and I played in the Silver Gardens. Where my mom sang me songs of the angels."

I close my eyes, picturing his words in my mind. "Tell me about your home. The house you lived in."

"It's… it's hard to remember." He chuckles, but it's not a happy sound. "Gifted with immortality, but no great memory. There are only flashes left. Only dust I try to grab in the wind. I remember… I remember a palace of white and gold. I remember spires that glow like the sun. I…" he grows teary, then swipes at his eyes. "I'm sorry."

I squeeze his hand. "We all miss home."

He smiles. "Thank you. For helping me remember."

"Asher, let me go home. Let me go home back to Fen."

He looks at me deeply, a great sorrow lurking in his eyes. "Sometimes, we can never go back."

3

LOST CITY

Fenris Vane

"Fen is a good man, but he is myopic in his focus."
—Kayla Windhelm

Her blood pumps through my veins, like fire and ice. My demon mark burns with her call, a demanding pulse that beckons me, drawing me forth, through the layers of fresh snow and ice, through the carcass of winter left behind by the storm.

I am not a man accustomed to fear, but I feel it now, filling me with its poison of doubt. What have they done with her? What will they do? What if I never see her again?

Kayla lays a hand on my arm. "I see the worry on your face, brother. Ari is strong. And if they wanted her dead, they wouldn't have gone to such lengths to keep her alive."

My half-sister is not wrong, but it does little to temper my rage. I should have kept her safe, instead, she saved my life and risked her own.

I had hoped for some clues at Stonehill Castle, but of course there were none. And despite the refugees of my capital city swarming to the castle for safety and help, despite the chaos caused by battle and death, I left the moment I felt Ari call for me with blood.

Kayla insisted on coming, though I know she worries for her charge, Daison, who didn't make it out with the others. She worries for the people under my care. But she too loves Ari, I remind myself. She wants her safe and home almost as much as I do.

"There is nothing out here," Kayla says as we walk further into the wildness that is the outer edges of my realm. We are coming close to the Outlands, where rebel Fae likely gather to strategize their next move.

They must have her there, in the Outlands, on the edge of our world. Where else could they have taken her? Certainly not to one of my brothers—none of them would work with Fae. And if the raiders still have her in my realm, they are more foolish than even I have given them credit for. I already have what scouts I can spare searching my lands. With orders to kill.

The pulse in my wrist changes and I stop, looking around at the withered trees and old stones. "She's close." The white wolf at my side sniffs at something in the air and growls. I rest a hand on Baron's head. "Find her, boy. Find Ari."

He howls and leaps through the snow. Kayla and I follow behind. In moments, Baron turns into the mountain and disappears.

A cave, nearly hidden by snow-covered vines, is carved into the stone, and Kayla and I duck to enter, both of us pulling our swords out in preparation.

Baron doesn't waste time checking to see if we're following. He shoots through the darkness toward a destination only he can smell. Kayla flicks her hand, and a glow of soft white light appears before us, illuminating the darkness—she knows she can use her magic with me, if not with anyone else. We creep forward, Kayla's light and our enhanced night vision guiding us.

We travel through narrow passageways guarded by stalactites and stalagmites that threaten to impale us with one wrong move, until we reach a cavernous space with two towering blocks of rock standing as sentinels at the corners of a stone door. In the middle is a spiked imprint in the shape of a hand.

My mark blazes. She has to be here somewhere.

Kayla walks up to the door and examines the markings carved into stone. "This is Fae magic," she says. "Only a Fae can use this, I think."

"Do it," I say.

"I'm only half Fae, Fen. It might not work." But she puts her hand over the spike and shoves her flesh into the door until her blood covers the imprint.

Nothing happens.

I curse and punch one of the stone pillars.

"That's not helpful," Kayla says, tearing a piece of fabric off her shift and wrapping it around her bleeding hand.

I walk over and stick my own hand over the spike. I hear something, the faint sound of metal grinding, but then nothing. Using sheer strength, I attempt to open the stone door, but despite my considerable power, I cannot budge it.

"Go back to Stonehill," I command Kayla. "Put together a crew. Find Ace and get his help. Tell him we need something that can open this. I'll wait here. I will break down this door and dig my way to the center of hell to save her, if I must."

Kayla hesitates, and Baron glances between the two of us, waiting. "Fen... " her voice is soft. Conciliatory. And I know what she's going to say before she says it. "We don't even know where this door leads. If it leads anywhere at all." She lays a hand on my arm, as if to soften the blow of her words. "Let us research. Let us think this through. And let us go back to Stonehill. Your city is burned. Your people displaced. They've lost their home. Their loved ones. They need their prince."

"Ari needs me more."

...

I consider staying. But Kayla's words haunt me. What would I do alone in the cave? Beat my stubborn head against the stone waiting for it to break? I will be more useful in Stonehill, so I leave with Kayla, even as Baron dances in circles around the strange door, howling and growling and sniffing and wagging his tail in distress. He can feel her. Smell her. He knows they took her this way. But neither of us can crack the code of how this door opens or where it leads, so we have no choice but to head back to the castle. The sun is near setting by the time we return.

We walk through the city more slowly this time, taking in the damage. The burned houses and destroyed food stores and fallen trees. The bodies that litter the streets. The stench of burnt flesh that still lingers in the air despite the storm.

"We will need to put together work groups to collect and bury or burn the dead," I say as we walk.

Kayla nods, but says nothing.

Until she sees something within the ruins of a collapsed and burned building. She cries out and runs into the ash. I stop and wait, my heart heavy when I see her return with a charred body in her hands and tears running down her dirt-smudged face.

"It's Daison," she says. "He's dead."

"I'm sorry, sister." It is all I can say. Ari would know how to comfort her, how to share in her sorrow, but I have had to lock my heart against the cost of war, or I could never do what I do. Still, I understand. Her pain is raw, her grief deep. She raised that boy, trained him as her apprentice in blacksmithing, loved him as family. The wall around my heart cracks a little for her as we walk.

She carries the boy's body all the way back to the castle, and I set about having the city cleared. The vampire remains will be burned in funeral pyres, as is our way. The Fae slaves who died will be buried, as is theirs. The Shade can go either way, depending on their next of kin preference. Tonight, the sky will burn with the fires of sorrow.

I have Kal the Keeper send out six ravens, one for each of my brother's realms, with orders to hold a Council meeting immediately. I'll need their help if I'm to find Ari and pull my realm back together after the Outlander attack.

Waiting is the hardest part. I don't spend a lot of time in the human world, but I do envy their technology and rapid communication methods. A cell phone would be particularly useful right about now.

To stay busy, I make my rounds through the refugee camps that have formed within the castle walls. Funeral pyres have already been constructed, and many have begun the process of burning their dead and whispering goodbyes. Vampires don't much believe in an afterlife. We are immortal. If we die, that's the end. But Fae have different beliefs, of resurrection, of living beyond. The Shade often straddle the fence on what happens after death.

I stop at each ceremony, giving respect to the dead before moving on to the next. I ask myself what would Arianna do to help the people heal, and I try to offer her words, her kindness, through my body. It's not the same. She's so much better at this than I am, but it's the best I can do.

When I reach the pyre for Daison, I stop and stand next to Kayla. I do not touch her, or hold her, because I do not feel she wants those things. Instead, I offer her my strength silently with my presence.

She speaks an old Fae blessing and lights the flames to set Daison's body free. I'm surprised she chose the vampire way rather than Fae, and I tell her so, when it's over.

"He and I lived by the fire of the forge. It seemed fitting he should leave this world by fire as well."

I nod and then finally pull her into an embrace. Baron howls as the fires fade and the ashes are all that remains of Daison. Kayla weeps silently.

There will be many pits of ash this night. Many new graves dotting the landscapes beyond, some marked, others not.

Many empty homes and hearts that once were full.

And in the end, there will be more war. This is what I have wrought. I am the Prince of War. I am the Prince of Death.

...

Marco and Roco, two of my most trusted soldiers, intercept me as Kayla and I make our way back to the castle under moonlight.

"Sir, we need you in the city," Marco says. He has dark circles under his eyes and looks as if he's aged ten years in the last few days.

"What's the problem?" I ask.

"Lord Salzar is torturing and executing the Fae rebels captured in the battle. He has them strung up in the city center."

I curse under my breath. "By whose orders?" I ask.

Roco scowls. "By his own authority. He says he's supported by your own law."

Kayla and I turn and follow Marco and Roco back to Stonehill. The sounds of shouts and screams grow as we near the city center. A throng of people has gathered around the square, howling for blood. They spread apart before me, and we make our way to the center, where Salzar reigns like a king, his enemies hanging on hooks behind him. His face is red, and spittle flies from his mouth as he shouts to the excited spectators. "And what shall we do with this one?" He slashes a blood soaked whip into the air, and it tears open the back of a woman hanging before him. She is topless and fighting against her restraints. Her long blue hair is matted with blood and dirt.

"Gut her!" Someone screams from the crowd.

"Beheading!" Someone else shouts.

The suggestions become more and more gruesome, more violent and twisted. Kayla sucks in her breath beside me, and I know this sight must shock her.

Next to the woman, another man hangs naked. He is already dead, but it wasn't an easy death. His guts have been torn from him violently, and dangle from his limp body.

"Stop!" I shout in a loud, commanding voice.

The crowd falls silent, and Salzar finally notices me. A red cape falls down his back. His hair is short and black. He doesn't cower. He sneers. "Greetings, Prince

Fenris. So glad you could join us in exacting justice on the monsters who ravaged this realm."

"This ends now," I roar, working very hard to reign in my own temper. To refrain from bashing the man's face in with my fist.

The crowd grows uneasy at my words, whispering.

Salzar raises an eyebrow. "Would you deny the people their due victory? Would you spare the rebels who destroyed your city and killed your citizens? Are you not the Prince of War?"

There's a shift in the air. Everyone is listening, but they are unsure of who to follow.

Baron stands by my side, alert and ready for battle. "I am the master of this realm, Salzar. Not you. You have no authority here, and no right to decide the punishment of prisoners of war." My voice is low, but it carries through the crowd.

"They killed our families," Salzar says. His voice is compelling, passionate, a master manipulator riling the crowd's thirst for vengeance. "We cannot let our enemies live. You taught me that, Prince of War, when you killed my son for attacking your princess."

And now we come to it. I knew Salzar would be a problem, and he picked the worst time. Rodrigo deserved his fate after attacking and attempting to feed on Arianna, but this crowd will not understand why the

Fae who killed their families don't deserve the same fate. I'm losing control.

"Take the remaining prisoners to the Keeper," I command my own soldiers. "Get them food, aid and rest." The crowd is shocked into silence, then that silence breaks in a wave of outrage.

"Consider this," I say calmly, quieting them once more. "How do you want the Fae to treat any hostages they might have taken from our side?"

Salzar sneers. "They took no prisoners. All have been accounted for, dead or alive."

I turn to him, digging into him with my gaze, showing the wrath in my eyes. I walk up the steps of the stage, shaking the wood beneath my boots. "You're wrong, Salzar. They took one. They took Princess Arianna."

There are gasps in the crowd, a shocked pain that grows. I was counting on this response. In the short time Arianna has lived here, she has worked her way into the hearts of these people. They love her.

Salzar is at a loss, so I press my advantage. "You have already killed several hostages who might have had information about where Princess Arianna is being kept. Your reckless disregard for the authority of this realm might have cost the princess her life!" I can only hope my words are exaggerations meant to stir the emotion of the crowd, and not prophetic. "Guards!

Take Lord Salzar to the dungeons to cool his tempers and remind him who rules here. Three days should be sufficient."

Marco and Roco grab the struggling man and drag him through the streets as he shouts profanities and swears to end me. I would laugh, but there is still the matter of finding Ari.

"To the rest of you, focus your energies on rebuilding your homes, your lives, your city. The prisoners will be questioned, and I will find the princess."

I leave then, with Kayla and Baron by my side.

"Careful, brother," Kayla says, once we are out of earshot of anyone. "You cannot make too many enemies and still rule."

...

Word will get out now about Arianna being kidnapped, and my brothers will panic. I need to find her.

Now.

I storm back to the castle and make my way to the Infirmary. Kal is tending to three prisoners who are much the worse for wear. He doesn't have them chained to the beds, which concerns me. Marco and Roco stand guard, and I order two more men to join them in securing the prisoners and keeping Kal safe.

"I need to question them," I tell Kal.

"You can try, Your Highness. But they are not very coherent."

Kal is almost as tall as me, but more slight of build, with a long white beard and long white hair. He might seem old, aged, but for the unlined skin. He is ancient, however. Only Fae who live many hundreds of years or more grow hair so white. He is also someone I trust, despite his heritage and our current war with his people.

"Have they said anything useful?" I ask.

"No," he says simply.

I walk over to the woman who was being whipped when we arrived. She is moaning in pain, and I crouch next to her bed. "What's your name?" I ask.

Her eyes are glassy and lids heavy. She's too pale and clearly doesn't comprehend me.

I move on to the next prisoner, an older man with thick arms and chest and a bright red patch of hair on his head that falls to his shoulders. "Where are you from?" I ask him.

His eyelids flicker, but they do not open. He looks feverish.

The third man is entirely unconscious.

I sigh and walk back to Kal. "How long before you can have them healed enough for interrogation?"

Kal frowns. "It depends on how well their bodies respond to treatment. They were each badly wounded in the battle, and then tortured more after."

His voice is impassive, but I wonder what lurks beneath. Does he feel loyalty to the people he hails from? Does he abhor the violence perpetrated on them by my kind?

"Send for me the moment one of them comes to. If they know anything about the whereabouts of the princess, I need to know immediately."

Kal nods. He too loves Ari and worked closely with her over the last several weeks. She spent as much time in the library with my Keeper as she did in sword training with me and sword making with Kayla. It's astonishing she found any time to sleep.

As I leave the Infirmary, a messenger arrives with a scroll. The Council has been called. My brothers await my arrival.

...

The six of them sit around the great round table in the Council Chambers. Their respective banners, mine red, Asher's purple, hang behind them. Blue torches light the black marble walls. I take my seat in the great wooden chair carved with wolves and swords. "Arianna has been taken by the rebels. She used her blood to call

me through my demon mark, but it led to a dead end."
I explain about the cave and the door. "My people must
rebuild after the attack. I need forces from each of your
realms to help me defend Stonehill while I search for
Ari."

Levi snorts, flicking his long white hair away from
his eyes. "You? Brother, you were responsible for keeping the princess safe and you lost her. We need someone more capable to save the princess."

"I hate to say this, but I don't disagree," Dean
says. He wears no shirt. Not even to a meeting. "She
was meant to be mine this month, when you took her.
Now she's gone and I still haven't gotten my turn.
Maybe someone else needs to take the lead in finding
Arianna."

I growl at the two of them.

Niam stands and leans over the table, his eyes pen-
etrating. His head is shaved clean, his dark skin gleaming from his moisturizer. He is dressed in the finest
clothing money can buy, as always. Niam never lacks
for wealth or the finer things. "Stand down, Fenris.
They speak the truth, and it would be folly not to heed
them. You have a city to defend and rebuild. A war to
fight. You are needed to protect this entire kingdom, in
addition to your realm. And your month with Princess
Arianna is over. Let someone else take this mantel so
you can handle your own affairs."

How dare they? I will find Arianna with or without their help, this kingdom be damned. I will—

"*I* will find the princess," Asher says calmly. His skin is dark under the eyes. He must not have slept for many days. "I know her best," he glances at me, "outside Fenris, who has had the most time with her. I recruited her from her world. I brought her here. She trusts me."

Levi chuckles. "And why should we trust *you*? You, who always side with the Prince of War?"

Asher turns to face Levi. "Do you think Ari will go with you, Levi? After what you did to her during the presenting? Do you imagine she wants anything to do with you now?"

Zeb smirks and runs a hand through his short dark hair. "Asher has a point. You were quite an ass to her, and she's human, not Shade or slave. They have ideas about equality and such. She's not a fan of you or Dean at this point. I second Asher being the one to lead the search for the princess."

Ace has been quiet this whole time, lost in his own thoughts, no doubt, but he looks to me, nods once slowly, then turns his attention to the group. "I also vote for Asher. He's in the best position to find the princess and bring her home, allowing Fen to defend the realm and kingdom."

Levi, Dean, and Niam vote against Asher. It's three to three. I am the deciding vote. It's clear if I do not side with Asher, Levi or Dean may be chosen instead. I sigh. "Find her, brother," I tell Asher. "Find her and keep her safe." The 'or else' is implicit in my voice, and he nods. I know he understands, and even though he lost some of my trust with his recent lies, I do believe he wants Arianna safe.

Dean shrugs. "Fine, Asher will do. Just get me my princess. I have plans for her that I'm sure will change her mind about things."

The bastard laughs, and I growl.

Asher places a cautioning hand on my arm. "Not now, Fen. This isn't the time."

I turn and rush out. I care little what the Council thinks. I'm going to find the woman I love.

As I leave the room, Ace's voice stops me. "Fenris…" We're alone in the hallway, but I do not turn to face him, fearful of the anger I will spew.

I hear Ace step closer. He speaks softly. "I know where you're going. And I know why. But consider this, before you act rashly. Your people have fallen. They need their prince. What will you choose, Prince of War?" He steps closer. "Who will you save?"

4

THE DARKNESS

"When the demons came from the sky and slaugh-
tered the High Fae, the Spirits left us."
—Madrid

I stand naked in front of a full-length mirror in my bedroom. The Fae locked me in the same room as before, but this time, they removed all the drapes. My white robe lies in a pile at my feet as I consider what to wear today. My choices are limited to gowns in light blues and whites with soft flowing fabric. I hold up a blue gown, studying my reflection, then switch it with a white gown, when a man's voice startles me.

I spin around, covering myself with the white dress.

"I like the blue on you better," Asher says, not even bothering to hide his smirk.

I toss the blue dress on the floor and slip the white one over my head in a small act of defiance. I don't bother trying to be modest. Let him squirm. I'm not ashamed of my body.

He chuckles. "Reverse psychology. Works every time. The white is more striking."

My cheeks burn, and I want to hurl some insult at him, but he saved my life last night, so I guess I owe him... what? Courtesy? Maybe if he's nice.

I sit in the chair by the north-facing window, and he sets a tray down on the wooden table next to me. It's full of food and a goblet of wine. I nibble on fruit, nuts, cheese and bread, and then sip at my drink. It's light, sweet and refreshing.

"I came to make peace with you," he says.

"Didn't you already try?"

He chuckles and holds up bandages. "I also came to dress your wound."

I hold my arm out and he pulls a chair up to me and unwinds the bandage covering the claw marks left by the gryphon. I flinch as the bandage sticks to the dried blood.

"Sorry," he says, flinching with me.

He wipes it clean with a wet cloth and rubs a purple salve on it. "Looks to be healing well," he says as he wraps clean bandages around it. "Madrid could speed up this recovery with magic, you know."

I pull away once he's done and return to my food. "I don't need her magic. And I won't be here long, at any rate. I'll find a way to escape," I tell him.

He frowns.

"Is Fen well? Have you seen him?" I've been assuming Fen healed and felt the blood call, but I don't have any proof.

"He is angry, but alive, if that's what you mean."

I nod, comforted by that fact, and emboldened in my next statement. "You can't hold me here forever. Eventually, Fen will find me, and when he realizes you have kept me prisoner, he will kill you all." I say the words, knowing they are true, but I don't want anyone to die. I don't hate Asher, even if I don't fully understand what he's doing or why. And I don't want Fen stuck in the middle of a blood war with his brothers because of me. There has to be a better way.

Asher sits on the other side of the table and drinks deeply from his own goblet. "You're right. He will come for you. And while he can't reach you now, he won't give up. But you nearly died last night trying to escape. Are you willing to risk your own life again?"

"If I must," I say without hesitation. "I'm tired of being treated as a pawn in other people's games. As a dog expected to submit to its master."

He flinches when I throw his father's words back at him. "What if I can arrange for you to leave here and see Fen again? Without death-defying escape attempts or civil war?"

I tilt my head and pop a grape into my mouth. "I'm listening."

"Come with me to talk with my father, Madrid, and Durk. I have a plan, but you'll have to trust me."

...

"You propose what?" King Lucian's face contorts in displeasure. "This is folly!"

I bite my tongue and wait. Asher said I needed to trust him. I don't, not really. But I have to believe he can sell this plan to Lucian. It's my only shot. Still, my back is rigid as I rest my arms on the sturdy wood table we all sit around.

"She will live in my realm," Asher explains, "but she will return here regularly for training."

Lucian scowls. "And what if she doesn't return?"

"And what if she stays here but does nothing?" Asher leans forward. "Father, we need her cooperation, and as we've seen, we'll not get it through threats. We need a compromise." He sips from his goblet. "Arianna will continue spending time with the seven princes, thus fulfilling her contract, the one *you* insisted on. In turn, she will do what is needed here..." he glances at me, "without complaint."

I grin humorlessly.

Durk grunts. "The kid's got a point."

Asher doesn't look as amused at the title, but he wisely says nothing. I fight a smile at anyone calling an immortal demon 'kid.'

Lucian leans back in his golden chair, sighing. "This will abate suspicion from your brothers..."

"And," Asher adds, "It will keep the Prince of War from bringing his sword down upon the Fae while we try to make peace."

Lucian nods once, sharply. "Very well. But we will need a blood oath."

I scowl. "I've already signed one of your contracts, demon."

Lucian chuckles. "Then you will have no problem signing another." So, that's where Asher gets his wit.

The Prince of Pride glances between me and his father, his eyes nervous. He touches my hand with his, then faces Lucian. "She will sign... under certain conditions. The contract will end when she becomes Queen, or at any point if you or I choose to dissolve it."

Lucian glares at us. "I may dissolve it. No one else."

"No." Asher squeezes my hand tighter. "Either of us. Me or you."

The King clenches his jaw, silent.

"Father, you are in hiding, presumed dead. It is smart leadership to delegate someone in your place should you be indisposed to make important deci-sions." Asher waits, his expression plain.

I can't read him. I can't read his father. They are both cold.

Madrid leans over the table and stares at Lucian. "We sided with you because you promised peace, but right now the Prince of War draws near because of the princess. So far, you're not proving to be as useful as you promised."

Lucian sighs. "Fine. Draft the contract."

Asher smirks. "Already done." He pulls out a scroll, similar to the one I signed to save my mother, from somewhere in his cloak. I'm not sure if I'm happy or upset he already had one prepared.

Asher makes a few changes.

The king takes it and reads through the archaic writing.

I grit my teeth. We'll see whether I'll sign or not, but I don't want to argue with Asher here, in front of the king. I don't want to give Lucian the satisfaction.

"Very well," the king says, handing the parchment back to Asher. "But she must also be presented before she returns to Inferna."

I bristle at the idea of being 'presented.' It didn't go so well for me last time.

"Only if she is chosen," Madrid says.

"Chosen?" I look around, waiting for someone to explain, but no one says anything until Asher winks at me.

"You'll find out tonight."

The king nods. "If you are all in agreement, then I will concede to these conditions. But she must bind herself now."

Madrid and Durk nod.

Asher hands me the contract and the same pen I bled into before. I take my time to read each word, making sure I understand what is being asked of me. I can tell the king is impatient and wants me to sign immediately, but he can wait.

I note the most important parts: I won't be allowed to discuss my, Asher's, or Lucian's involvement with the Fae. I won't be allowed to share my knowledge of the king and his true fate.

"I want my sword back," I say. "Write that in."

Asher is about to speak, but Lucian cuts him off. "Fine. I care not."

I sigh and continue to read. "I want something in here that guarantees the terms of my original contract will still be honored, and that nothing you ask of me now will jeopardize my mother's health or well-being. I will still be allowed to return home. She will still be safe and cared for no matter what."

Lucian growls. "One contract cannot negate another. The first is still in effect. Even if my idiot son gave too much leeway in rewriting it."

Asher's face doesn't even flinch at his father's vitriol.

I smile and hand the contract to Lucian. "Then it shouldn't be a problem to include that here. If you want my cooperation?"

Lucian doesn't look like he wants my cooperation. He looks as if he'd rather drain me of my blood and be done with it. But Asher takes the contract from him and makes the changes, then hands it back to me.

"What happens if I break this?" I ask.

"You can't," says Asher. "If you try, you will find you are unable."

"Unable how?"

Asher squints. "Let's just say there's pain involved. Lots of pain. But, that won't be an issue, will it, my dear?"

I cut my arm and fill the pen with my blood, and for the second time in a month, I make a deal with the devil.

...

Spero is returned to me, and I place her—yes, she's a she—against my bed. Three young Fae girls arrive to bathe and dress me. There's a large tub in the corner of my room, and it is filled with hot water, oils and flower petals. I step into it and luxuriate in the heat and heady scent, closing my eyes as I try to forget for a moment where I am and what I must do.

I think of Fen instead. Sometimes I feel him with me, but when I turn to look he's gone. I know it's just my imagination playing tricks, but it feels so real that my heart drops each time I lose him again.

I wish he and Baron were here right now. I'm nervous about the "choosing" and "presenting." I tried to pry more answers out of Asher, but he disappeared with the king and said I needed to get ready for tonight. Apparently there will be a crowd to witness whether or not I'm chosen.

After my bath, one girl uses a pumice stone to buff the soles of my feet while the other two work on my nails. "You have a lot of calluses," the youngest looking girl with blue hair says.

"Sword fighting. And blacksmithing. Neither are easy on the hands," I explain.

Her eyes grow wide, and she looks like she wants to ask more questions, but the taller girl with red hair glares at her, and she stays silent.

I wish they would ask more questions, or talk. This silence is unnerving. I try to elicit some communication from them, but they answer all questions in curt mono-syllabic answers until I give up. I don't want to get them in trouble, and maybe they've been forbidden from speaking to me. I don't know.

My hair is brushed out until it dries and is braided into dozens of small braids that are then weaved together to form an elaborate design around my head, almost like a crown. Silver ribbon has been woven into the braids, and tiny crystals are added once the design is complete. It's striking against my black hair.

Rose oil is rubbed into my body before the girls dress me in a silver sleeveless gown dotted with tiny sapphires at the hem and neckline.

My make-up is classic: red lips and winged eyes. The younger girl adds final touches of silver dust to my face, chest and arms that makes me glitter under the right light. The tall girl slips my Blue Goldstone ring onto my finger and steps back.

"You are ready," all three say together, then they bow and leave the room.

That wasn't weird at all.

I sit on the edge of my bed, waiting. Presumably someone will be coming for me.

It feels like hours pass before the sun begins to set and there's a knock at my door. I stand, impatient for something to happen.

Asher smiles when I open the door, and appraises my appearance. "You look astonishing."

"I've looked astonishing for about three hours." I frown at him, fist on hip. "Why did I have to be ready so early? Do you know how hard it is to not mess up a dress or make-up this fancy? The struggle is real, dude."

"Indeed," he says dryly. "Are you ready to go?"

I nod and take his arm when it's offered.

He's dressed in a white suit and cape with blue and silver accents, and while he looks astonishingly handsome, I don't tell him so. The Prince of Pride doesn't need encouragement.

We walk across a bridge that links my bedroom to a huge tree, our outfits billowing in the strong wind. Within the center of the trunk is a winding staircase we take to reach land. Madrid, Durk and the king all wait below, everyone dressed in shades of white, silver and blue. Sky and air colors to represent their element.

A retinue of guards dressed in white formal uniforms escort our group across the floating island, between silver trees and homes carved into stone. Snow crunches beneath our feet. A bird sings from atop a tower. As we travel, Fae on the street begin to follow us, whispering amongst each other. Some even leave their homes to join the crowd. They come in groups of two or three, then five, then ten, until I can no longer count how many.

It's clear they were expecting this. They are all dressed formally in Air colors. Many carry white and silver feathers like bouquets. The path we walk sparkles in the moonlight, lit with candles and glowing orbs of light that float around us.

We finally arrive at our destination: a grand tree so tall it blocks the sky and so wide you could drive a car through it. It reminds me of the California Redwoods, except this tree is silver, the bark, the branches, even the leaves. Asher brings me to stand before the trunk, where a hollow is covered in tangled roots. In the middle is a handprint spiked with silver.

"It is time for the choosing," Madrid says in a loud voice so everyone can hear. "Blood alone will determine if Arianna is truly heir to Avakiri."

The crowds raise their hands and a breeze blows through the night, catching my dress and swirling it around my ankles.

Asher takes my hand and places it on the handprint. "You must give it blood," he says.

He steps back, and I look at my hand, pale against the silver of the tree, my ring the only splash of color with its deep blue stone full of sparkles.

The spikes are deep, and the pain flashes up my hand, wrist and arm as blood trickles into the tree.

Nothing happens.

A hush falls over the people watching. Waiting. The wind around me dies down.

Beads of sweat form on my forehead and under my arms. My skin feels hot, sticky. My body aches. I want to pull my hand off the spikes, but instead I push further into the pain, imbedding the silver thorns more deeply.

Everything is quiet. Too quiet. As if the whole world has disappeared and I am the only one left.

My hand burns. I try to pull it toward me, but it's stuck. My ring tightens. The stone grows larger. It's so heavy it tears at my finger.

Then my vision goes black, and I can no longer feel anything but weightlessness.

I float in a sea of stars.

There is no gravity. My dress drifts around me as if in water. I can't see anything but the bright points of light around me. I hear nothing. No.

There is something. The swishing of air. Movement.

The darkness takes shape. Small at first, then larger. It grows legs, claws, a tail, spikes. Wings sprout from its back, spanning into eternity. The darkness turns to me, its face reptilian in feature, but with a consciousness much deeper than any lizard. It stares at me with eyes like stars.

"You are mine," a voice whispers in the darkness. "You are the chosen." It is loud, all consuming, layered like a chorus. It is soft and hard at the same time. It is gentle and furious. Not female or male. Something else. It surrounds me. It embraces and engulfs me.

"You are the Midnight Star."

My head fills with visions of life and death, visions that flash like fire before my eyes, and my ears feel pulled, stretched, torn from my head. I spin in space, and white light explodes from within me.

Fire and ice fill my veins, remaking me into something new, unlocking ancient secrets stored deep inside my cells.

"Go now, child of midnight," the voice says inside me. "Awaken the wilds."

...

The ground is hard beneath me, and my body buzzes with a new energy. Heady. Unsettling. A hand reaches for me, helping me to my feet. Asher. He stares at me, his eyes wide, his jaw slack.

"What's wrong?" I ask. "Did I fail?"

My head throbs, and I can't take in all the people staring at me just yet, so I focus on Asher's eyes, on his hands holding mine.

"You most certainly did not fail, Princess," he says with awe in his voice. "On the contrary, I fear you've succeeded."

Madrid steps toward me, a secret smile on her lips. She nods her head and one of the guards brings over a tall silver mirror, placing it before me. "See for yourself," she says.

It takes a moment to realize I'm looking at myself. Before me stands a Fae with black hair tinged with blue sparkles. Her ears are pointed. I am no longer Arianna, the human girl from earth. I'm something else entirely.

I study the rest of my reflection. A black dragon armband coils around my right arm. It's warm on my skin, and when I reach out to touch it, the band moves, uncoiling its long tail and raising its head.

I gasp, staring at the band, first through the mirror, then directly as it leaps into my hand, its small wings fluttering in the sky. It's the color of my new hair, dark blue—almost black, with bright stars moving through its scales. It's the size of a kitten. A baby dragon. The color of midnight.

I glance down at my finger, where my mother's ring once rested. The silver band is still there, but the stone is broken, cracked open like...

An egg.

I look into the creature's eyes, and it makes warbling sound, "You're Yami," I say.

His lips curl, like he's smiling, and he hops on my hand, chirping.

Asher and Madrid stare at me, frowning. I hold the baby dragon up to them. "Was this supposed to happen?" I ask.

Asher squints "I'm not sure..."

Madrid shakes her head. "Princess, we do not see what you are seeing."

I look down at Yami and back up again. "This dragon. It hatched from my ring."

Madrid's eyes widen, and she bows. "The Midnight Star has been reborn." Other Fae fall to their knees, bowing, but most look on as skeptically as Asher. Lucian scowls from beside the tree.

Madrid's words trigger my memory, of my transformation in the dark starry night. "Midnight Star. Yes. The voice said I was the Midnight Star. But why can't you see Yami?"

The Fae looks at my head, her eyes focusing until she smiles. "He is an ancient spirit of our people, and only reveals himself to those he chooses. I believe, yes, I saw him, for a moment, but he is gone again. He has just been reborn, and you are like his mother. It will take time for him to grow accustomed to others, to grow strong again, just as it will take time for you to master your own magic."

Asher grimaces and looks back at the glowing silver tree. It looks more alive now than it did when we arrived. My blood seems to have revitalized it.

"Is something more meant to happen?" Everyone still seems to be waiting for something, as if me turning into Fae and hatching a dragon from my ring wasn't enough of a show.

Madrid's words are low, meant only for Asher and me. "Now that Yami has returned, the other Druids will awaken. Within this tree sleeps the Air Druid and his spirit. We are waiting for his slumber to end."

"What happens when it does?" I ask.

Asher sighs. "What indeed? Old sins will be revisited, undoubtedly."

Madrid glares at him. "Ignore the vampire. When the Druid awakens, he will teach you how to master your magic and help you find the other three Spirits, so that we might unite the four corners of our kingdom once again."

Lightning flashes in the dark sky and hits the silver tree, filling it with light. I cover my eyes with my hand, squinting in the glow.

A hush falls over those who came to see this magic unfold. The tree groans, and the silver roots that covered the hollow begin to pull away, until a dark opening appears. Yami jumps to my shoulder and perches by my ear, nuzzling my neck and hair and purring. He too stares at the tree.

Asher sucks in his breath as the shape of a man forms against the shadows, stepping into the light.

He is dressed in white robes, his head bald and tattooed. His eyes are such a pale blue they are almost white.

He's beautiful. Mesmerizing.

He looks at us a moment, then stares at Asher.

"Hello, old friend," he says in a low voice.

"Hello, Varis."

5

HIGH FAE

*"But your blood is the most powerful, that of the High Fae, that
of the royal line. You are heir to our lands, heir to Avakiri."*

—Madrid

A buzz sweeps through the crowd, but rather than
escalating, it moves in a wave as the Fae closest to us
become quiet. The silence spreads, and all I hear is
the shuffle of feet, the brush of fabric against skin, the
subtle movements of hundreds of Fae pushing in closer
to us.

Varis and Asher stare at each other, speaking more
than words with the looks they exchange. They have
history, that much is clear. And not all of it is good.

It's a reminder to me of just how long these people
have lived. More lifetimes than I can imagine.

Yami perches on my shoulder, nuzzling against my
neck, hiding under my hair as dozens of hands reach

out for Varis. The Fae grip his robes, and a circle forms around him as the people who can't reach him touch those who can. Their numbers grows. All the Fae in sight grip the person in front of them, all connected to the man who walked out of the tree.

A flurry of wind picks up around us, carrying on it a new, spicy, scent. The darkness of night comes alive with a soft glow. It radiates from Varis and into the crowd, spreading, growing, until everyone glows silver.

"What's happening?" I ask Asher under my breath.

"He is a kind of god to them," Asher says. "The Old One. The Wild One. The Air Druid. He is sharing his power with his people to show he has truly awoken."

Madrid stands next to us. She touches the person in front of her, and her face glows. "You will inspire this reverence as well, Ari," she says softly. "When the Midnight Star is revealed, when you are presented to our people, you will become a god to them."

...

Her words weigh heavy on me as I am escorted back to my room by Asher. It seems the Fae will stand around the tree all night, and I need to rest for tomorrow, for training and presenting. I sit down on my bed, and Yami falls asleep curled around my neck. I rub his back as he snores into my ear. "I don't want to be a god to these people," I tell Asher, who sits in a silver chair.

He looks mildly amused. "Why ever not? Isn't that the ultimate elevation? To be worshiped by all?"

"Have you never paid attention to history? Mythology? Heroes only stay elevated for a time. Then their people turn on them and kill them. Mortal gods never live long in any stories I've ever heard," I say.

He frowns, his brow furrowing as he considers my words. "I can see why that wouldn't be optimal. But this is different. The Fae revere the High Fae and the Wild Ones. You are both. They wouldn't dream of turning on you." He stands to leave, promising to retrieve me in the morning for training.

"And what will I be learning?"

He shrugs. "It is for the Druid to decide." Before I can ask more, he leaves, closing the door behind him. He exchanges words with my guards, but I can't make out the what they are saying. Footsteps fade.

I uncoil Yami from my neck and place him on the pillow on my bed. He purrs softly in his sleep, seemingly happy, content.

I wish I could borrow some of that joy. Instead, I stand and walk over to the full-length mirror by my dresser. I slip off my gown and study my body. I still look like me in most ways. My body is the same. My face is the same. It is my hair and ears that make me something not human. I run a finger over my earlobe and to the pointed tip, exploring the new skin, new cartilage. I pull my hair out of its braids and study the deep blue that now shades the black. It sparkles under the moonlight streaming into my room, just like the ring that made Yami.

I walk back to my bed and study the tiny dragon sleeping there. It's a marvel that my mother's ring had been a dragon egg all along. Did she know? Did my father?

Tendrils of resentment unfurl in me. They did nothing to prepare me for my fate. They left me to deal with this completely alone.

They must have had their reasons. Someday I hope I will have a chance to ask my mother all the questions building up in me. Until then, I must try to rest. I blow out the blue candles and snuggle onto my bed with Yami. A moment later, something licks my chin.

"Yami?"

He keeps licking.

I turn away, trying to sleep. He starts to lick my hair.

Ah! The problems of being a Fae Princess, Wild One…

…

The next morning, Asher guides me outside, through a forest of silver trees and mist. A chill sweeps the air, and morning dew covers the shrubbery, glistening with an ethereal glow.

The Prince of Pride is silent as we walk, a rare occurrence, and I am too lost in thought to initiate conversation. Yami is with me, of course, perched on my shoulder, sniffing at the air in delight. I sense I won't ever be without him again. I can feel a tether to the tiny dragon. A spiritual chord that connects us forever. I'm not sure he and I could survive being apart.

"What does he eat?" I ask Asher, breaking the silence.

He frowns. "Who? Varis?"

"No, not the Druid. Yami. What does my dragon eat? I need to make sure he is cared for properly."

"Don't you just... know what to do?"

I roll my eyes. "Sorry, the library was out of 'How to take care of your new baby dragon.' And the movie wasn't helpful."

Asher smirks for the first time all morning, and I smile back, half-disbelieving how different my life is now. A month ago, I was a waitress at the Roxy, and now I'm the official Prince of Hell cheerer-upper.

Yami licks my cheek, unconcerned with our conversation. I don't know how big he'll get, or what I will do with him when we go to my world. I have so many questions.

Asher looks more closely, presumably trying to see the dragon that still does not wish to be seen by anyone but me. "Varis will tell you all you need to know."

"You know the Druid. Or at least, he seems to know you. Are you two close?" I ask.

Asher's face hardens, and he looks away, picking up speed. "We were friends long ago, but no longer." There's a finality to his words that make it clear he's not interested in talking further.

As the sun climbs in the sky, we arrive at a trail leading up a mountain. I can see I'll need to be in excellent shape to keep up with all this hiking and mountain climbing I've been thrust into. It's a good thing I had all that training with Fen and Kayla. I'm stronger than I've ever been.

Many minutes and breaks later, we arrive at the peak, snow crunching beneath our feet. A silver tree with a trunk so large you could fit a small house into it stands before us. There is an opening carved into the trunk, and Asher leads me through, into a large chamber edged by tangled silver roots. Sunlight streams in from holes in the top, casting everything in shades of gold. A pool of clear water rests in the center. A flat black rock juts out from the water. The Druid, covered in white furs and silks, floats inches above the stone in a lotus position. His eyes are closed, his breath steady.

Asher gives me a small bow, then leaves before Varis notices him.

I shift nervously from foot to foot, wondering what I'm supposed to do. Should I say something? Introduce myself? Cough to get his attention? At the thought of coughing, I suddenly need to actually cough, but I don't want to disturb what seems to be some very serious meditating going on, with levitation and everything. What if he falls from the noise? What if he bruises his tailbone on that black rock? All because of me? Could I be punished for causing damage to a god's ass?

I'm spared from further consideration on the subject when Yami leaps off my shoulder, flutters his wings and screeches so loudly I'm certain the entire Air Village can hear him. He stares at something above. A silver owl. Sharp blue eyes.

The bird glides down toward us, digging into the earth with sharp talons, spreading its large wings, appearing larger than it is. Yami leaps away, shriek-ing, eyes wide with fear. The spikes on his back stretch upright, and then he does something new. He erupts in blue flame.

"Silence!"

The Druid's deep voice fills the cavern, and both the owl and Yami freeze. The screeching stops, the flames die down. Yami seems himself again, and he jumps up and lands on my shoulder, digging claws into my flesh, eyes fixed on the bird.

I don't know whether to apologize or yell. So I just stand there, silently, waiting to see which direction this goes.

Varis lowers down onto the rock.

And he jumps.

No...

It is more a glide, as if he were lighter than air, and he lands in front of me, his feet barely making a sound. His white furs billow behind him. His tattoos, which I thought black, but now see are a deep blue, glitter in the light. A gust of wind drifts around us, though there should be no wind in this cavernous tree.

The ancient Fae looks at me, his eyes probing. "Arianna Spero, your spirit is untrained, young and impetuous. From what I've heard, he is much like you."

I bristle at that. "It is not through any fault of ours that we are young and untrained," I say.

A grin plays on his lips. "And impetuous?"

"Often an insult levied at the bold by those too set in their ways to take chances or seek change," I say.

He nods. "I heard many tales of you last night, some favorable, many not. It is good to see the truth of things in your eyes. It seems my people have indeed become too set in their ways to see the Wild One in you."

He flicks his fingers, and the owl lands on his left hand, gripping the brown leather fashioned there. "This is Zyra, my Air Spirit. She is ancient, wise, and... very proper." The owl flashes him a look. A frown? The eyebrows are very expressive. Varis grins. "It will be interesting to see how your Yami does with her."

Yami screeches at the sound of his name, and I make hushing sounds at him, hoping to soothe the spirit. "You can see my dragon?" I ask.

Varis nods. "He has shown himself to me and Zyra. But it is critical he show himself at the presenting this evening."

"He won't," I say. "No one can see him but you and I."

"That is why you must train. I will teach you how to harness and control your powers, how to wield your spirit for the greatest good. Are you ready to learn?"

I nod.

"Very good," he says, hopping back to the rock. "We will begin with the simplest of castings. That of Illusion. Madrid told me you will be returning to the Seven Realms. You will need Illusion to hide your true identity from the demons. This is a casting our youngest Fae learn as children, so it should not take you long."

...

Famous last words, Druid. Famous last words.

I am stiff, cold, tired and hungry, and still I sit in lotus, meditating on the 'ember within that burns with magic.'

There is no ember.

There is no burning.

There is no magic.

I'm beginning to fear I do not have enough Fae blood in me to be what these people need. I tell Varis, and he shakes his head. "Yami would not have come to you if that were true. I would not have woken. The ember is within you, but it is buried deep. We must bring it to the surface."

"If you say so." He and I haven't done much talking, and there is much I'd like to ask him about, but the training comes first, and apparently the training involves silence and meditating.

A bell sounds in the distance, and Varis stands. "That is all for today. You must return to your room and prepare for the presenting this evening."

I stand and stretch the parts of my body that have fallen asleep. All of them. Yami yawns and snuggles deeper into my hair. He slept through most of the day, lucky dragon.

Varis turns to the exit.

"Wait," I say. "What do I feed Yami?"

"Feed?" He raises an eyebrow. "I'm sorry. I forget how little you know of our ways. Yami will eat meat. He will eat a lot. Be prepared."

I glance at the little dragon, not quite believing Varis. "He hasn't had much food yet…"

"He is a spirit, but he has taken physical form. Soon, he will begin to crave physical things. Keep him fed and exercised. Oh, and he likes it if you tickle his spikes."

I try some tickling, and Yami purrs in his sleep. "Thank you, Varis. Will you be there, at the present-ing?" I ask.

He nods.

I fidget with my hands. "I won't have to undress, will I?"

He frowns. "Why ever would you have to undress for a presenting?"

I let out a sigh of relief. "Don't ask."

…

Madrid informs me the presenting will occur in the Crystal Palace, so we must fly back. Asher escorts me to Gryphon International, and says others will follow soon. It seems the golden gryphon remembers me, and I certainly remember him—particularly the sharpness of his claws. I climb on him gingerly, but soon find that I haven't lost my delight in flying. Yami wraps his tail around my arm and opens his wings, taking pleasure in the wind pushing against him as we soar. He never lets go of me though; it seems my dragon has yet to learn how to fly.

Once back at the Palace, Asher escorts me to my room where a staff of three await. Once again I'm scrubbed, pampered and dressed, this time in a silver gown with a long train covered in rhinestones. My hair is pinned and braided and curled until Asher deems it perfect, then he sets a small velvet box on my dresser. I open it and catch my breath.

He smiles. "This crown has been in your family for more years than you can imagine, princess." It's a delicate platinum circle of vines, with small leaves embedded with emeralds and accented with tiny sapphire flowers. He sets it on my head and weaves it into my hair so it doesn't fall off.

Yami coils around my neck, batting at one of my curls with his claw, his talons retracted. When my hair moves out of place, Asher glares at my neck. "It's the dragon, isn't it? Tell him not to muss up the perfection I have spent hours creating."

I laugh and pluck Yami off my neck, holding him in my hands. "You hear that, Yami? Behave or the big bad vampire might eat you."

Yami mews and crouches into a ball of tiny terror, as if to combat any evil thrown at him. I laugh again and

83

look over at Asher. "He's ready to destroy you with his might."

Asher rolls his eyes. "Destroy away, as long as he's ready to show himself tonight. The Fae must see him if they are to believe the Midnight Star has returned."

"What will happen if he doesn't?" I ask as he offers his arm.

"Best hope we don't have to find out."

...

The ballroom has been transformed into something out of a fairytale. No longer is it the crumbling remains of a palace long forgotten. Tonight it shines with floating lights and iridescent fabric, tables heavy with the finest of foods. White birds flutter above, perching on the black stones jutting from crystal walls. Smells of honey and spices and roasted meat for the Fire Tribe fill the air. Yami perks up at the smell of meat. The hall bustles with a diversity of Fae, some light skinned, some dark, some short and some tall. They part for us as Asher escorts me to the front.

"All four Tribes have sent representatives for the presenting," Asher says. "Fire, Air, Earth and Water. They are all here to see the Midnight Star."

"So no pressure then," I whisper back.

He smirks.

One of the Fae, a short man with a green beard, notices Asher and frowns. He is not the only one; all around, the vampire is met with glares. King Lucian's presence at the front does not go unnoticed either, with whispers of the monster king spreading through the room. Even I feel revulsion at seeing him here, clad in black armor, red cape flowing down his back, sitting in a golden chair next to the Crystal Throne, a place of honor, in the palace of the people he nearly made extinct.

Asher leads me to a platform before the Throne. He raises my hand to his lips and gives it a kiss. "Good luck."

As he walks off to stand by his father, Madrid strides up to me. She wears an intricate gown of silver, and blue gems hang from her neck. She raises her arms at the hundreds of Fae gathered below. "I present to you, Princess Arianna, of the High Fae, returned to us at last. She has been chosen, and through her blood, has awakened the Wild Ones, the Old Ones, the Five Spirits. Rise, Fae of the Four Tribes, rise and greet your future Queen."

I face the people, and watch as they all stand. The unison of their movement thunders through the hall. "She is half human!" Someone shouts from the crowd. "She is not fit to lead us."

Another Fae agrees. "Her blood is not pure."

The crowd roars. "She communes with vampires!" "Where is Yami?" "She is false!" "This is no—"

The giant stone doors to the ballroom crash open. They have been opened by one man. Varis. He stands at the entrance, his white furs swaying in an unnatural wind. His tattoos glimmer in the blue light. Zyra sits on his left arm, glaring at the Fae who have all gone silent. They face the Druid, eyes wide with awe. Many of them have not seen a Wild One in centuries. Some have never seen one at all.

The Air Druid walks forward, a gust of wind pushing against everything in his presence: plates, jewelry, cloaks, even men and women who draw too close stumble back. His voice echoes amongst the crystal. "I have been awoken by the blood of the Midnight Star, the blood that flows through her. She is High Fae. She is our true ruler."

The crowd turns back to me, eyes curious, even... hopeful, and I know what they're waiting for.

Yami.

I nudge the dragon on my shoulder. "Come on, Yami," I whisper. "These people love you. Care for you. Show yourself for one moment. That is all they need. That is all *I* need." My eyes sting with tears as I imagine what Lucian will do if I fail tonight. My body recalls the ache in my ribs from his blade. "Please, Yami. Please, for me."

His eyes go glossy, and he looks as near to weeping as me. He scans the crowd, their silent faces, the way they collectively lean forward to be closer to him. And then he jumps down in front of me. He walks forward on the pedestal, and I know in my heart he will do this. He will do this for me. "Thank you, Yami—"

"What does it matter?" booms a voice, rough and harsh.

Yami flinches, skittering back, hiding behind my dress.

A new man, larger than any Fae I have ever seen, stands in the entrance, his body covered in red and gold armor. A white powder of sorts, maybe ash, paints his hands and forearms. His beard is burgundy and reaches down to his waist. Dark red tattoos swirl over his arms and neck and bald head. A Druid.

"What does it matter if she is High Fae?" His voice is low, rumbling, powerful even when quiet. "They failed us before. And they will fail us again."

Varis steps toward the man. "Oren, please..."

Oren glances at Varis, studying him, and sneers. "Who is it that led us at the time of the Unraveling? Who is it that lost battle after battle?"

"The High Fae," someone yells.

Oren walks forward, addressing the crowd, bones knitted into his beard and jewelry rattling with each step. "The High Fae." He stops, and glares at me, his dark red eyes burning with rage. "The Midnight Star."

Madrid rushes down the pedestal, standing between me and the Druid. She lifts up her hand. "Oren, please…"

For a moment, the Druid's eyes turn soft, but then he looks away. "I will not follow the High Fae again. I will lead my own war against the demons. Who will join me?"

Agreement moves through the crowd. "I!" "And I." "I will join you."

A new voice, soft and cold like freezing water enters the hall. "And I." A woman saunters into the ballroom, her long turquoise gown rippling behind her. Her skin is dark, covered in silver tattoos. Her head is bald. A light blue and green serpent, its body scaled, its teeth long and sharp, twists around her right arm, slithering up and down in her grasp. When she speaks, a chill flows through the room. "We have been awoken. What other need is there for the Midnight Star?"

Whispers move through the crowd.

Varis frowns. "Metsi, this is not our way—"

Metsi's serpent snaps at the Air Druid. Metsi chuckles, petting her snake on the head. "Now, now, little one, where are our manners? This foolish man doesn't deserve such hate."

She walks past Varis, standing beside Oren at the base of the pedestal. "We will keep the Midnight Star safe. But she will be no leader."

Varis dashes to their side, his face full of anger, the wind roaring around the hall. "Yami is the one who binds us. He is life. He is death."

"He is weak," says Metsi. "The Yami we knew died in the Unraveling. What is he now?" She glances up at me, her eyebrows curious.

She wants me to summon Yami for all to see. I tremble, my hands covered in sweat. My mouth is dry. Yami sits under my dress, shaking against my leg. "I... I..."

Oren laughs. "She can't even control him." He points at me with a giant ashen finger. "Take heed girl, if you do not tame the spirit, it will tame you."

He turns back to the crowd, and pulls a ruby necklace from behind his beard. He whispers to the gem, and it begins to glow. The floating lights flicker and glow brighter. Oren holds out his hand and snaps his fingers. They spark, and from the sparks erupts a bird of red flame. It sits on his arm and roars.

"I am Oren, Druid of the Flame, Keeper of Riku, Spirit of Fire."

The dark skinned woman lifts her right arm, and her serpent screeches, spikes standing up on its back.

Water begins to float around the hall, leaving goblets and bowls. A man drops his plate, trembling at the clear water filling the air before him. A streak of wine glides past me, and I run my hand through it, tearing it in two. The serpent snaps at me.

Its master smiles. "I am Metsi, Druid of the Waves, Keeper of Wadu, Spirit of Water." She turns to the crowd. "Join us. Tomorrow, we march on the demons."

The Fae roar with rage and bloodlust.

A gust of wind shoots through them, knocking men and women down to their feet, quieting all. Varis jumps, gliding through the air, and lands on the pedestal beside me. "What does Lianna think of this? You are but two of the five."

Lianna. The last of us. The Earth Druid.

Oren shrugs. "I have heard no news of her. Nor do I see her here. Apparently, she was more clever than I, not honoring this charade with her presence."

Varis frowns, glances at the door, seemingly hoping for the final Druid to arrive. No one comes. He points to me. "The Midnight Star unites us. Unites the Four Tribes. And she will bring peace between us and the demons."

Oren spits at us. "How can you speak of peace, when my own sister is a slave to vampires? We cannot make peace with monsters." He points to Asher. "Why does this one still live?"

A silence fills the room, and a nervous edge. The rage in Oren's eyes fills his body. He won't let this be. He—

I run for Asher.

Oren throws his arm forward, flinging Riku at the prince. The phoenix becomes a streak of flame, bright as the sun.

I leap to the side, pushing Asher out of the way, throwing myself in front of the blaze. The heat singes my skin. Blinds my eyes. My lungs burn. My tongue tastes ash.

And then...

Cool. Soft wind. Fresh air in my lungs. I open my tearing eyes.

Varis stand before me, a flurry of wind exploding around him, keeping the flame at bay. "Will you really fight here, Oren, in the Crystal Palace? Where is your honor?"

The flame dies down. I check on Asher, laying under me. His skin is smooth. Not charred. Not burned. Not like Daison.

My body collapses, tears pour out.

He holds me, whispers words of calm, his breath cool against my skin.

I raise my arms. They are pale, clear. I too am safe.

Oren sees us. He roars with rage. His ashen hands blaze with fire, his eyes glow red. "Where is *your* honor,

Varis? Siding with our killers. With our slavers. With those who came to our peaceful world and destroyed it!"

Varis says nothing. But the wind picks up. Harder and harder. Oren begins to slide back. He scowls, raising his arms.

Metsi touches his shoulder. "No more, brother."

Oren looks from Metsi to Varis, from me to Asher, from Durk to Lucian. His hatred grows in his eyes.

And then he looks at Madrid.

"Very well," he whispers. He drops his hands, and the fire dies, his phoenix fizzles, turning to a pile of ash at his feet. He and Metsi walk to the door, but once more, Oren turns back. He turns to the crowd, but I can see, he looks only at Madrid. "There will be war," he says. "Which side will you be on?"

6

RIKU
Fenris Vane

"I am Oren, Druid of the Flame, Keeper of Riku, Spirit of Fire."
—Oren

Slumber does not dull my senses the way it does humans. I hear her, smell her, sense her, before she knows I'm awake.

She is of the water. She smells of salt and sea, of fish and wind. No one can sneak up on the Prince of War while he slumbers, not even a Druid.

I turn and study her, standing by my open window. Her dark skin gleams in the moonlight. Ritual tattoos cover her bald head. A green-blue snake coils around her arm.

"You have one day to free all the slaves in Inferna," she says with her lilting accent. "Or we will invade and destroy the lands here and beyond. Yours, your brothers, and the next and the next until all demons are extinguished."

I spring forward, my body leaping across the room with the speed and agility of my kind. It should have been enough to catch her, to immobilize her, but she dematerializes, turning into mist and disappearing through my window.

My hands grasp at wet air, and I grunt in frustration. Baron stands by my side, howling into the night, as frustrated as I am that our prey escaped.

The Druids have returned. But how?

I write messages for my brothers, asking for reinforcements, but disclosing nothing else, lest the papers find their way into the wrong hands. I dress in grey furs and leather boots, hand the messages to Marco at my door, and head to the library, where I know Kal will be.

He sits by candlelight, reading a thick tome with rough pages. The old Fae never sleeps.

I take the seat across from him. It doesn't take long to tell him what happened. When I'm finished, I ask the most important question first. "How is this possible?"

Kal is thoughtful, tugging on his long white beard as he considers. "There is only one way to awaken the Druids," he says in his Fae accent, which always seems thicker this late at night. "With High Fae blood."

Rage and fear flood me at his words. I know of only one source of High Fae blood in this world.

Arianna.

Since she was taken, I have warred with myself over the right course of action. Defy my brothers and search for her myself, thus abandoning my people, or trust Asher and fulfill my duties.

But in the end, if I left my people to rot, Arianna would not forgive me. She loves them too much, so I focused on my kingdom. Asher knows the consequences if he fails.

I turn my attention back to Kal. Ari is in more danger than I realized, and I am beginning to regret my choice.

Kal does not blink as he holds my gaze. And I know he knows the truth about Ari. Perhaps he knew before me. Perhaps he's always known. But I cannot be distracted by those thoughts. Arianna could be in danger. She could be dead. There is no telling what they've done with her. "Arianna, she is—"

"A High Fae," Kal says, confirming my suspicions. "But why bring her to Inferna?" he asks.

"I do not know, but that is the ultimate question, is it not? I believe my father sought to unite our bloodlines. High Fae and the Fallen, bound by blood. I believe he sought peace between our lands."

Kal frowns and pinches the edge of his nose. "If he did, he failed. This will only bring war."

I nod. Even Kal, a Fae, understands things aren't so simple as my father would have liked us to believe.

"Will you free the slaves?" Kal asks after a time.

I pace the library, my thick boots echoing off the stone floor. "I cannot let them go. I have already lost the support of many of my people. They will rebel if I do this. Something my father never understood. You cannot change everything overnight and expect your subjects to follow without revolt. Without consequence. Change does not come easy for the immortal, if it comes at all."

Kal nods.

All this talk with no solutions makes my head pound. There must be an answer without war. I must find Ari. "Are the prisoner's coherent yet?" I ask, an idea forming.

"Follow me, Your Grace."

Kal leads me out the library and to the Infirmary, a white-stoned place of little decor, dimly lit, where the prisoner's lay in their beds, well-guarded. "Though they are able to talk, they are not yet willing to," Kal says.

"They will find words tonight," I say, rage building in me. I walk into the room and find the largest, most dangerous looking prisoner of the bunch. A huge Fae with bulging muscles and a defiant face. I pull him out of bed and push him against the wall. "Where is Princess Arianna?" I ask him quietly.

The other prisoners look on with caution.

The big one glares at me, just as I expected. "I won't tell you anything—"

I kick him in the knee. Hard. So hard his bones break and his leg bends backward, unnaturally. He collapses into a heap, screaming.

The other Fae tremble in their beds. One, a young lad, pees himself, staining the white sheets yellow.

I turn to them. "Tell me where they have taken the Princess, or you will share his pain."

A young woman speaks up, the one I saved from further torture. "If we found her, we were to take her to a cave in the mountains, one with a stone door, I can show you."

"Where does the door lead?" I ask.

Her lower lip trembles and a tears fall from her eyes. "I don't know."

I cannot afford to have sympathy right now. I draw my sword and point it at her neck.

Her face fills with dread. "I swear by the Five, I do not know. I do not know."

I study her trembling, crying form. She is full of fear. Desperation. But no deceit. Why would she tell me about the cave but keep the rest a secret, at the cost of her life?

I turn to the others. "Anyone else know of the door?"

They shake their heads. The young man says, "Someone was waiting there to collect the princess, that's all we know, honest."

"There is one more thing," whimpers the woman. "I heard the commanders talking of it one night over wine. A spy. A spy in the Seven Realms."

I grip my sword tighter. "Who?"

"I heard no name. But they're in an elevated position, know all sorts of things."

I glance at Kal. It can't be him. I will not entertain the idea, but what if...

I sigh, lowering my sword and returning it to the scabbard. It seems only a few know of the door's purpose, and I've yet to find them.

I turn to Kal, whose face is impassive. "Tend to the man's knee. Have the rest fed and bathed."

He bows. "I can assure you my lord, I am not the—"

I grip his shoulder. "I trust you Kal. Be certain in this, and go about your work." Without another word, I march out of the castle.

Baron follows me, his paws leaving large prints in the snow. Wolves howl in the night, but he does not join them. He is set in his purpose like me.

We find Kayla by the forest, where a team of vampires, Shades, and slaves work to cut trees for the rebuilding of houses. A giant pine falls to the ground, shaking the earth. Kayla orders a Shade to load small logs into a wagon pulled by giant black horses. Her voice is calm, but assertive, delivering command after command.

"How are things progressing?" I ask her.

She shouts an order to tie down the logs to the wagon, then turns to me. "Well enough, despite the cold. The men are bringing up an invention Ace created. Something that should help us move the wood faster. We will have the city rebuilt soon."

"No," I say, my brain spinning with new plans forged from threats. "You must instruct everyone to build fortifications along the rivers."

Kayla stares at me, her eyes wild. "Forts? We defeated their army. Now is the time to rebuild."

"You will do as I say," I growl. "The Fae will return, and we must be prepared." I want to tell her about the Druid's threats, but she must stay focused on her task. All my people must. Telling them now will only distract them and hurt us in the end.

Thunder rumbles in the distance. It is a bad enough time to build as it is, but if it rains…. My people must be at their best.

But Kayla is not an idiot. She sees the worry in my eyes. "Have you learned anything from the prisoners?" she asks, arms crossed over her chest as she side-eyes me.

"They know of the door, but not what lies behind it."

She nods, looking lost in thought. "I wonder if..."

"What?"

"Nothing." She waves her hand in the air dismissively. "I thought I remembered something, but... it's nothing."

I nod. "Very well then. Transport the wood to the rivers. I will contact you later with further plans."

I turn with Baron at my heels and head back to the castle before she can respond. She knows something is off, but this isn't the time to question me.

Back in my room, I set to building a fire in my hearth. My servants have all been sent to aid in rebuilding, leaving me alone to tend to myself. I enjoy the silence, the peace, the solitude. Or I would, if the threat of the annihilation of my people wasn't hanging over my head, along with the loss of Arianna.

I undress, knowing I must rest, as I've barely slept since Arianna was taken.

A screech freezes me. Loud, all-consuming. Outside.

I run for the window, my stomach coiling.

I am the Prince of War. The Prince of Death.

But when I look outside, I know fear.

A phoenix blazes through the sky. Its wings span bridges. Its claws are large enough to tear apart a house.

It cries out, a high screech, full of malice and dread, and I know my entire kingdom can hear it. Tonight, they will all look upon the sky, and they will see fire.

The phoenix dives over the forest. The forest where Kayla and my people work.

It glides over the tall trees, sparking them with red flames.

Setting the forest on fire.

Men and women yell and scream and run to fetch water.

But they will not contain this raging inferno.

The world burns.

And our hope burns with it.

7

REMEMBER ME

"Yours is the sign of Lucian."
—Kal'Hallen

We make a sorry lot, spread throughout a barren hall. Most of the Fae left quickly after the Druids. Asher and King Lucian stand in a corner, engaged in a heated discussion. Twice I have heard them shout my name.

Madrid sits alone at a table, drinking straight from a bottle of something that glows blue. Varis is gone, not seen since the disastrous presenting, and here I am, drowning my sorrows with Durk of all people.

He's less annoying when both of us are drunk.

I hold my goblet up and tap the side. "It's empty," I say. He nods somberly and refills my wine, topping his off as well.

"At least no one tried to tear my clothes off this time," I say as I drink deeply from my cup, the flavor burning my tongue.

Durk raises a bushy red eyebrow. "You are royalty, regardless of what the other Old Ones say. No one would dare touch you in such a way."

I raise my goblet. "I'll drink to that."

Our glasses clink, and we drink. My head spins. Everything feels fuzzy and less important. Less weighty. I know this won't solve my problems, but it's nice to be out of my head for a few hours, even if I'll likely regret it in the morning.

"I'm not breaking any drinking laws here, am I? This is more like Europe, with a younger drinking age?"

He frowns at me. "I know not this Europe, but you are the law."

"Right."

We toast again. For I am the law.

I hear a hiccup and turn to see Yami lifting an entire wine bottle to his mouth. I grab it from him before he drowns himself. "You are definitely too young for that!"

He mews and drops his head, giving me big sad eyes.

"Nope. No wine for you. Come here."

Yami jumps back onto my arm and climbs up to my shoulder. I place the wine bottle a safe distance from

103

us, noticing the dragon licking his lips and tilting over a bit. There's a stain of red on his mouth.

I sigh. "Great. My baby dragon is a lush."

Durk shakes his head. "The Midnight Star does not sound as formidable as he once was."

"He's a baby," I remind him. "He will grow out of it." I hope.

No wine bottle in site, Yami glances at a platter of meats and cheeses. He dives off my shoulder, head first into the food. His claws push aside the cheese, and his little fangs tear into a slice of pork. This must be the hunger Varis warned me about.

Durk grunts at the food—which disappears into thin air for all but me—and leaves the table abruptly, returning a few minutes later with a bottle of something that glows silver, and two small shot glasses.

He fills both and hands me one.

"What's this?" I ask.

"Magic," he says, downing his shot in one gulp. His entire body shakes, and he yells, and giggles, and then his lips curl into a pleasant smile.

I sniff at my drink, then copy him, taking it all at once. I nearly gag. It burns down my esophagus and I choke, grabbing my throat, looking for something to put out the fire inside my body. I can feel it eating away at the lining of my stomach!

Durk guffaws and slaps my back, then pours us each another.

"You've got to be kidding," I choke out, still panting and waving at my mouth.

"Only way to tame the beast," he says.

I do another shot, and my world wobbles. Durk smiles at me, and I swear it's the first time he's looked at me with something other than revulsion or disdain. "You might not be as bad as all that," he says.

"Thanks, I think."

Yami returns, the platter empty of meat, and sniffs at my drink. He makes a gagging sound, then runs back up to my neck and hides behind my hair. I giggle uncontrollably and Durk frowns.

"Do ya know why this matters?" he asks, his voice low.

I stop laughing and look at him. "Why what matters?"

"This!" He waves his arms in the air as if to encompass everything. "You. The Midnight Star."

"I know why it matters to me," I say, thinking of peace, of Fen. "Why does it matter to you?"

"I had a younger brother once. Nat was his name. I remember a time we were little, playing by the gryphons. He wanted to ride one and I didn't stop him in time. Nearly broke his neck, and our mother nearly broke my bum after that. I swore I'd never let anything bad happen to him again." Durk sighs and takes another shot, and I wait, silently. "He was taken captive long ago. Taken by the vampires. I don't even know if he's dead or living as a slave. But he is the reason I helped start this rebellion. To find my brother. To bring him home, or put him to rest once and for all."

I think of all those Fae held captive by the vampires. By Fen. I reach over and place my hand on Durk's. "I'm so sorry."

He nods. "So you see, this is why you are important to me, Midnight Star. I do not want war. I want peace, a world where I do not have to fear for my family. And you are the only way I see."

I force a grin, though inside I do not know how I will ever succeed. Yami will not listen to me. The Druids will not follow me. And Lucian... I still fear what the king will do if he decides my worth is gone.

I look over at Madrid, who is still drinking alone, her silver gown dirty with specks of dust and wine. "What about her? Why is she so sad?"

Durk pours me another shot. "Long ago, Madrid and Oren, the Fire Druid you met tonight, were Karasi—spirit of the heart. She has waited for his return for many, many years. But Oren made her choose: You—the Midnight Star—or him. She chose you."

Maybe it's the liquor, or the disaster of an evening, but his words break me. She sacrificed her heart to do what she thought was right. I can't even imagine the strength it took.

I stand, excusing myself from Durk, and walk over to Madrid. I sit across from her, at a table full of uneaten food, stained with spilled wine.

"Hello, Ari," she says, forcing a flat smile onto her tired face. "I'm sorry tonight didn't go as we'd hoped."

"Don't worry about that," I say. "Are *you* okay?"

She looks about to answer with a polite yes, but then her face collapses into grief. Her eyes well with tears and she takes a sip of her glowing blue drink. "I apologize for showing so much emotion. It's unseemly."

I hold open my hands, an idea forming in my mind. Yami hops into them. "I think we can help her, Yami, what do you think?"

Yami looks over at Madrid, then back at me. Hoping he understands, I focus my intent on what I want him to do. "Let's give her some love."

Yami hops off my hand and walks slowly over to Madrid. He studies her face. He glows brighter, his body more clear.

And I know he has shown himself.

Her eyes widen and all the pain and sadness is erased from her face. "I... I can see him!"

Yami reaches for her hand and licks her fingers. He climbs onto her shoulder and purrs in her ear. Madrid's face is euphoric. Tears fall from her eyes, but they are tears of joy as she gently pets Yami's back. "Thank you. Thank you, Yami." She looks up to me, her eyes full of wonder. "And thank you, Princess Arianna."

...

The next day, my training begins with the world's worst hangover. I blame the glowing silver stuff Durk served me. Or maybe it was the glowing blue drink I shared with Madrid. Either way, lesson learned. Don't consume beverages that glow.

Since we are no longer in the Air Village, we have a new training location: a bridge of black stone spanning an underground chasm. Deep below us, magma floats in a river of red.

Varis sits across from me in lotus, drawing symbols into the dirt with a stick. "You look tired. Go back to your room, rest."

"I'll be fine," I say mid-yawn.

"Leave. I have no time to train someone unprepared."

I straighten my back, crossing my legs into lotus. As much as I would like to sleep, I would like to learn Illusion more. I need to before I can return to the Seven Realms. "I'm not going."

I expect Varis to bark more commands, but instead he grins. "I am glad to see you are committed." He whispers something, and the symbols he drew between us turn into a pool of water.

I gasp, seeing my reflection in what was just dirt a moment ago. "How?"

"You will learn in time. First, the illusion. Do you remember the incantation?"

I nod, closing my eyes and focusing. With my thoughts clear, my senses heighten. I hear Yami licking his claws, hear the magma groaning below. And I feel the aches in my body. My head pounds. My limbs are tender. I am not strong enough to do what Varis asks. And if I fail... I remember Lucian, how he sneered at me last night. I haven't seen him since—

Zyra swats my face with her wing. "What the—"

"She wants you to focus," says Varis. "And so do I. Clear your mind."

I sigh, take a deep breath, and speak with conviction. "*Celare!*"

Nothing happens.

"Concentrate," Varis says.

"*Celare!*"

Nothing.

"*Celare! Celare! Celare!*"

Nothing changes. I groan. Varis insists I keep trying. We spend the next hour practicing, but all it accomplishes is a sore throat.

The Druid paces at my side, his brow furrowed. "I am missing something…" he mumbles under his breath.

Zyra frowns, shaking her head.

I feel like an utter failure.

"Yes…" Varis mumbles. "Perhaps…" He sits beside me. "Let us try something different. Why do you wish to hide your Fae features?"

I think about it a moment. "Because the vampires don't like Fae."

He shakes his head. "You don't care about their opinion of the Fae."

"The contract," I say. "I have to fulfill my contract. I must hide my knowledge of the Fae."

"Only because the contract forces you. Go deeper."

I nod and focus inward the way he taught me, closing my eyes, shifting through my thoughts. Yami perches on my shoulder, his breathing calm. He seems to understand that we have to make this work. We are running out of time. Asher has told me Fen is growing more and more desperate to find me. If we do not return soon, he will find Avakiri and bring war upon these lands.

I must go back for the Fae.

For Fen.

I don't know how far his betrayal spans, if at all, but I owe him a chance to explain. And I miss him. I miss him more than I can think about.

"*Celare*," I whisper.

I open my eyes and suck in my breath.

My reflection has changed. My ears look human and my hair is black. I touch the tip of my ear, and it doesn't even feel pointed. Amazing.

Varis smiles. "What did you think of?"

I look to the distance, where an opening in the stone leads outside, where snow and wind dance. "Someone I care about. He is on Inferna, and if I can bring peace between our two lands, then I can keep him safe."

...

I walk through a dark cavern, heading to my room, Yami perched on my shoulder. A cold draft blows past my dress, the chill seeping into my bones. And I feel that sense of dread again.

Someone is following me.

I walk faster, my heart drumming, my palms sweaty.

The blue torches flicker and cast a twisted shadow. The shadow of a man.

Lucian emerges from the darkness. "I like you better this way," he says, studying my black hair. "Less Fae. More vampire. More like my wife." He raises an arm, reaching for me.

I step back, my hands curl in fists, my nails digging into my skin. "What do you want?"

His arm falls. His face goes cold. "To tell you I am leaving. Because of your failure during the presenting, I have other matters to attend to. Matters that will take me far from here."

"Good."

He smirks. "Have you considered why I did not make you my bride?"

My eyes go wide. If marrying him was the only way to save my mother, I don't know what I would have done.

He chuckles. "Do not fear. It is too late for that. I was so pre-occupied with securing my lineage, my legacy, I failed to consider what a... beauty, you would become." His words drip like poison. He strides over to me, touching my chin with his finger.

I push his hand away. "You disgust me."

"I understand," he says coldly. "You're so beautiful, so young and fresh, but when I remember what you are..." he raises his hand, holding it over my head like a claw. He shakes with a rage. His eyes gleam with dark desires. "When I remember what you are, my entire being fills with hate. I want to rip off your face. I want to imagine you are an insect, and when I step on you, I kill your entire race."

I shuffle backwards. "But I thought you wanted peace."

He laughs, and runs a long nail down the wall, and the eerie sound it makes echoes. "I will tell you something, Princess. Something I have told no one else." He turns to me. "I have no interest in peace. No. There is something else I am after. Something much more precious."

I step back. "What?"

His eyes flash to my shoulder, where Yami bats at my hair. "The Spirits."

I clutch the dragon close. He shakes in my grip. Lucian is more dangerous than I feared. I lean against the wall and prick my hand on a sharp rock. My fingers trace the rough stone. "Why?"

"For that, you will have to wait. But I assure you, in the end, it will be glorious." His eyes stare into the distance, into a vision only he can see.

"Why tell me this?" I ask.

He grins, humorlessly. "Because the High Fae once took something very precious from me."

A moment. "Your wife."

"Yes. And I want you to know, that one day, I will take something special from you as well." He looks again in the general direction of Yami, a hunger in his eyes.

"I'll tell Asher. I'll tell everyone."

"Try. Try to call out."

"Asher, I—" Pain grips my throat. It burns my lungs. I fall to my knees, choking.

Lucian steps forward, his shadow a giant over me. "Remember, Princess. You signed a contract. You may not share what you know of me." He smiles. "You may not speak of anything I do."

I tremble, the magnitude of my mistake crushing me. "I—"

Lucian grabs my hair, yanking me up against his armor. His face is close, his breath heavy on my face. He runs a hand down my cheek. "Now Princess, perhaps I will take what I desire—"

"Is something wrong?" Asher appears beside us, his eyes serious.

Lucian lets me go. His eyes glimpse what I drew on the wall with blood. Asher's mark. "Nothing, my son. I was just saying goodbye." He turns to leave. "Remember me, Princess. In the end, when you think everything you set out to do is done, remember me."

He fades into the darkness, and I fall to my knees and weep for the fool I was.

8

HOME

"You can look now, Princess. Welcome to hell."

—Asher

Asher holds me. For what feels like hours, he holds me. When my crying stops, he finally speaks. "What happened?"

"Your father—" my throat burns, my mouth snaps shut.

Asher trembles. "What did he do?"

"He—" The pain is too great. I bite down on my tongue.

Asher falls back, his eyes wide with realization. "I was a fool. I proposed that contract, and now..."

"Dissolve the contract," I say. "Do it."

"No. Lucian will feel it. He will know something is wrong, and he will return. No. We must wait. We must get you back to Fen. Perhaps one day, I can dissolve it, but… we must be careful. My father, my father is a dark and devious man. He has played this game of deceit and lies far longer than I."

I manage to stand, the pain fading. "So we do nothing?"

"No." Asher stands and grabs my hands. "We unite Inferna and Avakiri. Unite the Fae and vampires. Then nothing can stop us."

I pull back my hands, trembling, a new realization filling me. "If I marry you… this can really happen. We can really have peace. But…" My thoughts drift to Fen, to his arms around me.

Asher grins, and does something I will be forever grateful for. "Now, now, Princess, don't get too hasty," he says. "We must get to know each other first, after all. I do believe it is my month to spend with you." He offers me his arm. "Ready to go back to hell?"

I wipe my eyes, smile, and take his arm. "Definitely."

He guides me through the cavern and into a small cave lit by blue torches. This is not the path I first traveled to reach Avakiri. "How many secret elevators to hell are there?" I ask.

He chuckles. "Enough. Before Inferna was hell, it was simply the other half of the Fae kingdom. The Four Tribes were spread over both sides of the world, Avakiri and Inferna, and these elevators connected them easily."

"There must have been a lot of Fae back then."

Asher frowns. "There were. And we slaughtered them." His eyes go dark. "My people were thrown to this land like wolves thrown upon sheep. We did not understand our own carnage, our own bloodlust, until it was too late. One day, I will find the one who sent us here. And I will make him pay."

I touch his hand. "Your uncle."

He nods. "He stripped us of our wings, cursed us with a lust for blood, turned us into beasts, and unleashed us upon a peaceful people whose blood was an addiction to us. He doomed the Fae. He doomed us all."

"You had wings?"

"Once, yes."

"You… Fen… you were angels?" It fits the mythology, but it's hard to picture the vampires flying.

"All of us who were banished here—those of us who are the Fallen—once had wings." He smiles mischievously. "But we were never angels."

We arrive at a stone door covered in markings. I stick my hand on the spiked imprint in the center, and my blood fills the ancient runes. The earth shakes and the door slides open, groaning in the dark. Dust falls from the ceiling as we enter.

Yami chirps on my shoulder and begins flapping his wings. He floats into the air, staying near. Aw. My little baby is learning to fly.

He lands back on my shoulder, grinning.

I dig into my pocket and pull out a cheesecloth holding bits of meat and feed him small slices. The Fae weren't happy about preparing meat, but when Madrid convinced them it was for my invisible dragon, they relented. Or rather, they found a Fire Fae to do it.

Asher looks at me calmly. I think he is used to me interacting with thin air now. He warns me when we are about to flip in the center of the world. I put away the meat and grab Yami, holding him close. "Steady now, buddy."

We float in the air, and I twist so that when gravity returns I don't land on my head. My stomach wobbles and Yami shrieks, but we land down fine. I don't vomit this time.

The stone door opens, and we exit into another cave, this one with no lights. Asher guides me through the dark, his night vision much better than mine. We walk out into the light, into soft grass and flowing trees. There is a chill in the air, but it is mild compared to the Air Village or the Realm of War. Frost covers the leaves and bushes, but there is no snow. In the distance, a white castle draped in purple banners glitters in the sun.

Asher smiles. "Welcome to my realm, Princess."

"How? Isn't the Crystal Palace below Stonehill?"

He leads me forward, onto a cobbled path amidst a field of grass. "More or less. The Waystones, what you call elevators, do not travel straight up or down. They move at angles, allowing one to travel multiple places from regions like the Crystal Palace."

I nod, wondering at the genius behind these devices. Were they built by the Fae? Or are they even older?

Before I can ask, a carriage appears on the horizon, made from dark wood, the wheels coated gold. "Ah," says Asher. "Our ride."

We meet the carriage on the road. The driver, covered in a dark green jacket and hood, says nothing. The horses, two giant black stallions, try to nip at me.

Yami snaps back, growling.

I pat his back. "It's fine, little one. They don't know any better."

He keeps growling.

Asher sighs. "I am sorry, Princess. I was not the one to pick out these steeds, I assure you…"

The carriage door pops open. A young Fae girl with a short purple bob cut and a pristine silver dress that clings tightly to her body—likely picked out by Asher—jumps out. "Master," she says, her voice high and gentle, her Fae accent strong. "I brought the carriage as requested. I—" she trips on her sparkling high heals, muddying her dress.

Asher groans. "Hello, Seri. Allow me to introduce Prince Arianna."

I hold out my hand.

Seri stares at me. Then shakes my hand quickly as if it were a snake. "Pleased to meet you, your Highness, Grace."

Asher sighs. "Seri, please send out messages to my brothers. Tell them I have found the princess and she is safe in my realm. She will stay here for the next month."

"Uh, so a message for each prince, or one for them all or... " She pulls out paper and a quill pen and attempts to take down notes, but the paper bends over in her hands.

Asher speaks very slowly. "Six messages, one for each prince."

"Right," she says, biting her lower lip. "And you want them to come see Princess Arianna?"

"Bloody hell, no. Are you mad? That's the last thing I want. Just inform them she is safely returned to the Seven Realms. Do you understand?"

She nods and scampers inside the carriage to write. Sobs permeate outside.

Asher sighs dramatically and rubs the bridge of his nose. "My new Keeper. Her grandfather, my previous Keeper, passed away suddenly. She is his unfortunate, and only, replacement."

"She'll improve," I say, knowing all too well how it feels to be new at something. "And remember, she just lost her grandfather. She's probably still grieving."

Asher cocks his head. "I hadn't considered that. I thought she was weeping because of her failure to please me. But it makes sense now."

It's my turn to sigh. "You princes could afford a lesson or two in empathy."

"Yes, well, be that as it may, I still need her to perform her job adequately." He brushes his hands together as if to cleanse himself of unpleasantness. "Are you ready for the grand tour of the best realm in the kingdom? After all, it will be your home for the next month."

"Sounds lovely," I say, and Yami perks up at the idea of seeing new places. "But... will Fen be coming soon?" I don't want to make Asher feel bad, asking about Fen, but now that I'm back, I want nothing more than to see the Prince of War and make sure he's okay.

"He will be on his way shortly, no doubt. There's no point heading north to him, when he'll likely be heading south to see you. Two ships passing in the night, that would be. He'll be here before the day is out, with our realms adjacent to one another."

Asher's pleasant attitude puts me at ease, so I nod, and he helps me into the carriage. Seri stifles her crying beside us, focusing on the messages. The driver clicks at the horses, and the carriage begins to roll.

In moments, we enter a city full of platforms and bridges. Canals run below and around the polished stone buildings, the water full of boats large and small, transporting vampires and Shades. At the head of a small vessel a man with blue hair plays a violin and sings a haunting melody in a minor key. The scent of fresh flowers carries on the wind. The carriage stops, and we exit before a grand castle with towers that shoot past the clouds. Green vines sprouting purple flowers crawl up the marble stone, and ancient glyphs cover the colorful stained glass windows. Asher throws up his hands. "Welcome to Sky Castle."

He guides me forward, past giant opened gates decorated with eagles. Past gardens cultivated with immense care and detail, the shrubbery trimmed into the shapes of dragons, wolves, and eagles, the leaves purple, pink, and green. Giant flowers sway and dance in the gentle breeze. A perfume scent tickles my nose.

Yami hops off my arm and forges ahead, sniffing at the gardens and exploring all the new sights and sounds. It makes me nervous, him on his own, but I remember no one can see him but me. I suppose he's safe enough.

The dragon jumps into a rose bush and chirps loudly. I rush forward, lean down, and pull him out, pricking my finger on a thorn. Yami licks the wound.

Asher inhales deeply. "Best not to bleed in these parts, Princess. Fen may have strict rules about how his vampires feed, but we are more lenient here. And you smell delicious."

"Do I smell... Fae?" I ask, realizing I never did anything to cloak my scent.

Asher pauses. "You smell different, but not Fae. According to Fen, your blood doesn't have Fae properties either. Perhaps because you are half-human."

"How is my blood different?"

Asher smiles. "Fen said it did not have a toxic effect, but was still... addicting."

I wrap my finger in a bit of cloth from my pocket, stopping any bleeding. Yami perches on my shoulder, eyes wide and alert; seems jumping into thorns was enough exploring for him.

"This way, Princess." Asher guides me out of the garden and to a canal. A large wooden boat rests on the water, draped in purple banners, Fae and vampires bustling on the deck. We climb aboard and take seats near the back. "This is my personal barge," Asher says, reclining. "From here, we can explore my entire kingdom in comfort." At least a dozen slaves on either side of the boat begin to paddle oars, and we drift through the water.

"Why don't you use magic to power this boat?" I ask, eyeing the slaves with discomfort.

"A barge this size would require too much magic," Asher explains casually, as he leans back with eyes closed, the sun on his face. "And as you've seen, my new Keeper isn't the most reliable with her new tasks. This was easier."

"Easier? Having slaves work for you was easier?"

He squints open his eyes to look at me, a reply ready on his mouth, when two Fae girls bring us grapes and wine on silver platters.

"Kara? Julian?"

The two girls Fen assigned me in Stonehill Castle bow. "Your Grace," they say in unison. Kara beams, her golden hair shining in the sun, her dark eyes more tired than I remember. Julian, with her red hair tied in a bun, her green eyes full of life, fills Asher's goblet with red drink.

The Prince of Pride grins. "I thought you would feel more comfortable with them here. I was informed you own their contract."

"Yes... well, technically I suppose... " I smile at the girls. "How have you been?"

They curtsey. "Very well, Your Grace. We have been well cared for while you've been... gone."

"Good." There's more they're not saying, but I'll talk to them later in private. I want to know how the slaves I bought are doing as well. And I want to know about Fen. Slaves often hear and see things others don't, so they should be able to tell me much. I thank Asher for considering my comfort and bringing them to his realm.

He nods, a twinkle of flirtation in his eyes. "Anything to make M'Lady more comfortable. I want you to experience all the joys and pleasures this realm can offer."

I chuckle, sipping the wine. "Very well then. Let's enjoy." I turn to the Fae girls. "Go and relax for the rest of the ride. I don't need anything right now."

They bow and leave, finding some pillows to sit on while we travel.

Asher tsks at me. "That wasn't a good idea, Princess."

I lean over and whisper. "How can you speak of peace between the vampires and Fae and still use slaves?" The slave presence here is much stronger than in Fen's realm: slaves on the water, on the land, rowing boats, pushing carts, cleaning streets. I realize the Prince of War may be the most civilized of all his brothers.

"To keep up appearances. To keep up order," Asher says. "My father tried to free his slaves. And look what that got him. We must be careful. Even your small act of compassion has consequences. Look at the other slaves." He points at two men rowing the barge near the back. They scowl at the girls who now lounge in chairs across from them. From time to time, they glare at me. "They will resent the girls now, and resent you for showing them preferential treatment."

I bow my head. "This whole thing is ridiculous. You're right, but you shouldn't be. I'll be more careful. But there has to be a way to help some without making the situation worse for all."

He scoffs. "When you figure that out, let me know."

"I suppose it's what we're working toward, you and I. It's why we will unite the—"

The boat shakes beneath our feet. I drop my plate and cup, and they shatter on the deck, staining it red. The slaves look around, confused, but not yet scared.

"We hit something," Asher says, standing.

Two guards, clad in silver and purple armor, look over the side of the boat. Yami flaps his wings and flies around my shoulders, screeching. It's the first time he has stayed airborne so long. I try to calm him without drawing attention to myself. I realize I have to be more careful. The Fae know I have a dragon, even if they can't see it. But here, no one can know about Yami. It would mean danger for us both.

The wind picks up, blowing my hair in my face. It escalates, growing into such a crescendo of force that loose chairs and tables are thrown from the boat. Waves rise around us.

"What's happening?" I ask, peering over the edge, but seeing nothing but dark blue water.

Asher looks around, but his eyes are distant. "I have seen this before. Long ago." His voice is soft, barely a whisper. "Wadu."

The boat shakes.

A shriek fills the air.

I grab onto the side of the barge to keep myself from falling. Something. Something in the water. A grey snake. It slithers up from the canal. No. Not a snake. There are no eyes. No mouth. It is a tentacle. Swaying in the wind. Its movements slow, graceful, hypnotic.

It lunges forward.

I duck out of the way.

The tentacle hits one of the guards. It twists around his torso and shoots back into the water, pulling him into the deep.

Everyone screams.

The slaves grab weapons, oars, cutlery, anything they can find. I draw Spero, my sword, and hold it in a defensive guard. Yami clings to my neck, shaking. From behind his chair, Asher raises a blade of black steel, a thing greater than I can carry. A purple stone glitters in the pommel. "Arianna," he says. "Get to safety."

I stand my ground.

"You cannot fight this enemy."

A woman—a vampire—runs to the side of the boat. She is fast, ready to jump.

I scream at her. "Don't touch the water!"

Too late.

She dives.

She touches the waves.

And a giant silver claw erupts from the depths, piercing her entire body. It pushes her upward, where we can all see her bloody corpse, and then pulls her down into the canal.

No one else runs to the edge of the boat.

"To the center of the boat!" Asher yells. "To the center." The slaves do as he commands. Asher and his remaining guard join them. I follow. "Stay together," he says. "Do not—"

The ship shakes again.

I fall to my knees.

A tentacle flies over the deck, grabbing wildly, blindly. It clutches a man, the rower, the slave who scowled at me. Kara and Julian grab his hands, keeping the tentacle from pulling him to the depths.

But the tentacle tightens, and the man begins to choke. His face turns purple.

I rush forward and strike, slicing the tentacle in half with my blade.

The man falls back onto the deck, coughing uncontrollably.

More tentacles begin to rise at the edge of the boat. These are larger, thicker than a man. They will destroy this barge.

"Get off the boat," I yell. "All you who are Fae, go into the water!"

The man, who is no longer coughing, looks at me, confused. "But you said—"

"You're Fae," I say. "She's not after you. Once you're in the water, she'll see you. She'll recognize you and keep you safe. On the boat you're a target like us. Go!"

The man nods. "If you think so, Princess." He jumps into the water.

A moment passes.

A moment when I pray I do not see his bloody corpse float to the surface. A moment when I steel myself for what will happen next.

His head pops up through the waves, and he swims toward shore. I sigh, and laugh madly, my knees buckling under me. I was right. Wadu will not harm Fae knowingly. The man in the water is all the proof the other slaves need. They dive after him.

Kara and Julian do not join them. "We stay with you, Princess," Kara says.

The others slaves reach the shore. None appear harmed.

"Go," I say. "I'll be fine."

Julian nods, grabbing Kara and pulling her to the side of the boat. They jump into the water.

Something hits me from behind.

I fall to the deck, the air springing from my lungs. A tentacle, cold and slimy, wraps around me. The Water Druid will not care that I am Fae. She sees me as the enemy. As the one who will destroy her people by making deals with demons.

The tentacle yanks me to the head of the boat, my ribs crushed under the weight of the thick serpent. I stab at it with Spero, but my arm is weak. The air feels thin. I do little harm. Yami bites at the tentacle. His attempts do nothing.

From the depths of the water something emerges. A head. A serpent. Wadu.

Tentacles sprout like hair from the back of its head. Its giant mouth hangs open, sharp teeth dripping with saliva. It pulls me closer. Closer to its jaws. To the darkness I see there.

Asher jumps into the sky. Higher than I think possible. He flies past me. And rams his blade into the beast's eye.

The serpent roars, a primordial scream. The tentacles flail around. I am slammed into the ship. Again. Again. As the creature convulses in its rage. My head aches and rings. My body is splitting apart.

Asher clings to the beast's head, stabbing at its eyes, nose, fighting off the whipping tentacles as it attempts to strike at the demon.

Arrows fly toward the serpent, and I cringe, even in my own pain and panic, hoping none hit Asher. They miss the head and hit only the thick, scaled neck of the beast.

I must help him. I must help Asher.

I strike again with Spero. My hand is soft, my body feels heavy. I drop my blade. My vision fades.

Yami cries out, but it is a far away sound. So far away. And I strain to hear. I am tired. I am sleepy. Maybe, I can just rest. Yes. Rest. I close my eyes.

And then I hear it.

The sound that brings one last smile to my lips.

A howl.

Baron leaps on top of the tentacle and tears into the beast's flesh, ripping it apart. The serpent loosens its grip, and I collapse to the deck of the boat, air returning to my lunges in a painful burst. I choke, gag, and grab for my sword even as I try to clear my head and regain my wits.

A hand reaches for me.

A hand I have memorized.

A hand I have dreamed of.

I take it, and he lifts me to my feet.

"You know, you really should stop getting attacked by sea creatures," Fen says, his blue eyes so bright.

I try to laugh but it comes out as a croak. "Sea creatures should really stop attacking me."

He laughs, and the moment is too brief. There's still Wadu to deal with. But my heart feels so full, so complete with him here, that it's hard to muster fear or panic.

Maybe I'm still oxygen deprived.

Fen turns to the beast, his long brown hair whipping in the wind, his copper highlights catching the sun. "Asher!" His voice tears through the stormy air.

Asher sees his brother and hops back down to the deck. "Took you long enough," he says, grinning.

Fen grabs a long rope off the ship and throws one end to Asher. They look at each other knowingly, and nod. And then they charge in perfect unison.

They run to the front of the ship and leap into the air on either side of the beast, defying gravity once again, proving how inhuman they are. The rope catches Wadu on the neck and snaps tight. Asher and Fen use the momentum to swing around the beast from behind, tying the rope around the base of the head. The next time they touch ground, they land back on they ship, their places reversed.

And then they pull, moving backward as they do.

Together, they strangle the beast.

It roars and flails. It is not strong enough.

The brothers pull harder, moving further back.

The serpent wails. Its movements grow slower, more staggered, its mighty roars grow weak.

It is a terrible and wondrous sight, to see these brothers coordinate without words, without a plan, to move as one with such fluidity, grace and power. Their knowledge of each other is more profound than anything I've witnessed.

One more pull.

And the beast collapses, its head spilling onto the deck.

Fen and Asher exchange another glance. "Ready?" asks Fen.

Asher grins. "Thought you'd never ask."

They charge forward, swords drawn, and each blade takes the beast in an eye.

They rend their swords free, and the spirit, now motionless, slips off the deck and back into the water's depth, its body fading into mist.

The brothers clasp bloody arms, and the people on shore cheer.

Then Fen looks over to me, leaving Asher as he makes his way to where I stand in just a few long strides. His arms wrap around me and our bodies press against each other. I don't feel the pain of my bruised ribs or the shortness of my breath.

I just feel Fen.

"Welcome home, Princess."

9

SKY CASTLE

"There are no free Fae save for the Shade, and to call
them free would be to play with the truth. All Fae are
slaves to one degree or another in this world."

—Kal'Hallen

I can't let go of his hand, but we are all wet and
bloody, and my head is fuzzy. My knees weak. I start
to fall. Someone... Fen... grabs me. He carries me to
shore. I lean against his chest, listening to the steady
rhythm of his heart. He lays me down, studies my body.
Bruised and cracked ribs is the prognosis. He carries
me to the castle, to a room, to a bed. Women I have
never met before tend to my wounds, wrapping them in
clean bandages. They give me a thick elixir for the pain.
I fall asleep and dream of Stonehill, of the waterfalls
that rumble like thunder, of the rivers that turn rocks
smooth. There is pine on the wind and snow beneath

my feet. And there, in the distance, beside a frozen pond, stands Fen. I smile and hug him, and for the first time in a long time, I feel home.

...

I sit on a white bed, a fireplace crackling near me, purple curtains blocking most of the light. A thick rug decorated with an eagle covers the stone floor. This is my room at Asher's Castle. It is beautiful, but it feels too sparse, too foreign, to call home.

Fen arrives with Baron by his side. He is clean, his thick brown hair less messy than usual, and dressed in thin brown leathers, having dropped his furs due to the warmer weather. Baron wags his tail and lays his head on my lap. I nearly cry, seeing the big wolf again. I rub his head. "I've missed you, boy."

Fen smiles and takes a seat next to me on the bed. "He's missed you too. Wouldn't stop whining for you in fact."

I smile. "Was he the only one missing me?"

Fen holds my eyes. "What happened to you, Ari? You scared me near to death when you disappeared."

I want to tell him everything. About the Fae, about his father, about the contract, but the moment I try to speak, physical pain grips my throat. I choke and Fen hands me a glass of water.

"I'm sorry," he says. "You've just been through a significant ordeal. I didn't mean to interrogate you. I'm just glad you're back, glad you're safe."

I let him think it's my recent injuries causing the pain, because I can't speak the truth. But there is something I can try. "Fen, what really happened with your father?"

He pauses.

"Did you find the killer?" I'm hoping to get to the truth, to get him to talk about the poisoning. Maybe I can lead him to answers without telling him outright, thus circumventing the contract rules.

"I've been pre-occupied," Fen says, avoiding my question. He puts a hand on my knee. "There have been more important matters."

I smile, holding his hand.

Yami yawns, waking up from a nap on my shoulder. He hops down and roams the room, and Baron gets up to explore this new creature, sniffing his black tail. Apparently the wolf can see the dragon. Interesting. Does Yami only hide himself from people?

"Ari..." Fen leans closer. "There is something I must tell you, but I struggle to find the words. I..." He looks away.

I touch his face, turning it back to mine, gazing into his blue eyes. The world fades, and there is nothing but us, but my hand on his skin, but the breath between us. "Tell me," I whisper.

His voice is warm and soft. "When you were taken, it felt like my heart was ripped out. I can't lose you again. I won't."

I choke on the tears I can't shed. I want to ask him so much. Does he know I am Fae? Does it matter to him? There is one thing I can say though, that no contract can stop. "Fen, I thought about you every moment I was gone. I missed you so much it hurt. I don't know what we're going to do. I don't know what the future holds for either of us. I don't know how to handle the fact you don't want to be king and I must pick and marry the next ruler. All I know is I can't be without you again. I won't. Somehow we must make this work."

He looks about to say something else, when Baron licks Yami, and the dragon makes a trilling sound and bounces up and down, his wings flapping. The two have made friends.

Fen frowns, looking confused. "Why's he licking the air? Did you get knocked on the head, boy?"

There's a knock on the door, and Asher walks in, carrying drinks for us all. Baron bares his teeth at the prince, and I remember how much he dislikes anyone but Fen and me. And apparently Yami. "I thought we might want something stronger than juice after slaying a water spirit," Asher says, pulling up a chair next to us.

We each take our cups and I sip at my drink, hoping it doesn't land me with another hangover like last time.

It doesn't glow, so that's a good sign. "Is it really dead?" I ask. "The water spirit?"

Fen shakes his head. "The Spirits cannot be killed, not truly. Only injured. The best we can do is find the Water Druid. If she dies, Wadu will be forced to find another Keeper, to choose another Fae who is worthy. The spirit will be reborn, young again, weaker—for a time."

Asher nods. "I heard what the Fire Spirit did to your realm. My condolences, brother."

My eyes go wide. This is news to me. "What happened?"

Fen sighs. "Riku, the phoenix, burned our forests. We do not have the wood to rebuild Stonehill."

I remember Oren, the rage in his eyes, Riku the phoenix in his hand. I can almost feel the fire against my skin. "I'm sorry Fen."

The Prince of War grunts, looking at Asher. "You never told me, where did you find her?"

"In a village in the Outlands north of your realm," Asher says, lying with ease.

Fen studies me again. "And you weren't hurt?"

"No. I was held captive, but they weren't cruel to me."

"I felt you calling for me through the blood mark. I tried to find you, but it led to a dead end in a cave. An ancient door of some kind. Do you know of it?"

I look at Asher, unsure how to answer. I hate lying to anyone, but especially to Fen. It hurts more than any physical wounds ever will. "The Fae who captured me made camp in the cave for a while. They didn't seem to know what the door was either."

Baron howls and chases Yami around the room. I think the two are playing tag, and I stifle a laugh. Fen cocks his head. "I'll have to have him examined." He looks to Asher. "I'm going to need a room near Ari's, while she stays here."

I want nothing more than for Fen to stay, but Asher frowns. "Brother, your realm needs you now more than ever. And it *is* my turn with her. The others princes would frown on you being here. They would see it as an unfair advantage."

Fen bows his head. "I will need to see her again, Asher."

Asher nods. "I know, brother. I will make sure you do. But trust me to care for the princess. I won't let anything happen to her."

Fen stands, and I stand, not knowing what to do. Asher looks at both of us. "I have some business to attend to," he says. "The attack has caused damage I must help repair. Why don't you two say your goodbyes in private while I... attend to that business."

He leaves us alone and Fen reaches for me, pulling me into a longer, more intimate hug than on the boat.

I rest my head on his shoulder and breathe him in. It feels so good to be in his arms again, I don't ever want to let go.

"Have you healed well?" I ask. "I had to give you my blood. I'm sorry."

He chuckles and kisses my forehead. "Only you would apologize for saving someone's life at the cost to yourself. I'm fine. Thank you."

"Anytime," I say. "But you really should stop getting kidnapped and tortured by Outlanders."

He chuckles. "I've missed you, Ari."

"I still miss you," I say. "It doesn't feel like you're here, knowing you are leaving. When will I see you again?"

"Soon," he says, his voice low. "Soon."

Baron whines and pushes his nose between us. I lay my hand on his large furry head. "Take care of this guy for me, Baron, will ya? Don't let him do anything stupid." Baron licks my hand, and I pet him and then put my hands on Fen's chest. "We'll figure this out. We'll figure us out. But for now, go figure out your realm. Your people need you."

"They need you too," he says softly.

"Tell them I'm well, and that I miss them and my heart grieves for their losses. And tell Kayla... " My voice wavers. "Tell her I'm so sorry. So very sorry. I tried to save him. But I couldn't. I didn't know how, and it's my fault. I should have let her go. She would have known what to do."

"She doesn't blame you," Fen says. He lifts my chin with his finger, looking into my eyes. "No one does. It's war. People die."

"Don't die," I tell him. "I couldn't handle that."

"I'm not easy to kill," he says, grinning in his cocky way. "You'll be sick of me long before I die."

He leaves then, with Baron reluctantly following. Yami droops and makes little pouty noises as his new friend disappears out the door.

"We're both going to miss them, huh?" I ask. "I guess you don't get a lot of friends. Sorry about that." I walk to my new bed and sit down. "Are you hungry? Should I call for some meat?"

Yami wags his tail and flaps his wings, and I laugh and ring the servant's bell. Kara and Julian arrive, and I hug each of them. "It's so good to see you safe. Were you cared for well? Given a place to sleep and change?"

"Yes," Kara says. "Thank you."

"Could you fetch some food?" I ask. "I need a lot of meat. Raw, or as raw as you can get it." They frown at me. "I think I'm iron deficient."

That doesn't help. They exchange a confused look, then leave to fetch the food. I change into more sturdy clothes, black leather pants and shirt. Asher would say I'm supposed to be resting. Healing. And yes, my ribs still hurt, but the medicine I drank is helping. I do love the potions this world provides. Elixirs that can cure anything, it seems. It would be interesting to learn more about the medicines here.

When the girls bring back a plate of raw steak, I let them know I'm going for a walk, I won't need them for a while, but I'd like to talk with them later if they are around. They leave, and I feed Yami, who acts as if he hasn't eaten in his whole life, though I know for a fact he eats all the time these days. Once he seems satiated, he curls around my neck like a necklace and purrs. I grab a black and red cloak and leave the castle.

The temperature has dropped, as if Fen brought the cold with him when he arrived. I miss the Prince of War, so I look for something else to occupy my thoughts.

I walk around the city and admire the different shops. Most sell clothing and jewelry, Asher's expertise. Women walk in outfits of feathers and flowing silk, the kind I'd expect to see at a fashion show. Men wear dozens of rings on each hand, their necklaces heavy with amethysts and rubies. But I'm not interested in clothes and baubles right now.

Black smoke billows from a stone building, and I smile and walk toward the smithy. A large hammer sits on the counter, and I pick it up, enjoying the feel of the weight in my hand. With one touch it brings back a flood of memories, of Daison and forging iron, of laughter and banter and friendship. Of fire.

I drop the hammer.

A large man—the blacksmith—walks over. "You okay, miss?"

He doesn't seem to know who I am. That's good. I'd like some anonymity right now. "I'm fine, thank you," I say, even as my hands tremble. I try to distract myself. Something catches my eye to the left. A large white tent teaming with people. "What's going on there?"

"The healing tent," he says gruffly. "The new Keeper set it up to tend to those wounded in the recent attack. Heard they're looking for volunteers if you've got any skill that way. Nasty fight that was."

"It was at that," I say. I wish him a good day and walk toward the tent. The new Keeper, Seri, is there, her white dress replaced by a simple grey grown. She bends over a bed, tending to one of the guards injured in the attack. His leg is broken, bone sticking out from his flesh. Seri has men hold him down as she sets his leg back into place. He screams and I cringe, but the Keeper is unaffected. Calm, precise. She washes her hands of blood and moves onto the next patient, a Fae lad who broke his wrist in the water. In Asher's presence she was all nerves and more than a little incompetent, but here she is in charge.

I must admit I am surprised. "Can I do anything to help?" I ask.

She scowls at me, the tips of her Fae ears turning red. "This is no place for a princess." She pauses. Then adds, "Your Grace."

I grunt. "I've heard that before, but I'm a quick learner and not afraid of manual labor or getting dirty. I can clean, carry supplies, whatever you need."

She seems surprised at my tenacity, and cocks her head, studying me. "Very well then, we'll see how you do. Grab a bucket and start emptying out the chamber pots."

I nod and do as I'm told. It's smelly work, and not particularly pleasant, but I don't complain and that seems to impress her more than anything else. Yami, however, is not pleased. He sticks his head in one of the buckets and makes gagging sounds as he pulls out. I laugh and keep working, ignoring the awkward stares of everyone around me.

...

Time passes quickly in the Realm of Pride, as it is wont to do when one stays busy. My ribs heal in a few days due to the potions I take. I see Asher at dinner and sometimes lunch. He has work he's always off doing, and I spend most of my day at the healing tent. The Keeper finally begins to trust me and asks for more help. She even shows me different tools and their names, and eventually begins to teach me about the art and science of healing.

She shows me how and why to cut away rotten flesh, how to set a dislocated joint or broken bone, what creams to use to treat wounds and burns and how to make the simple ones. It's fulfilling work, and hopeful. Maybe if I learn healing, I will be able to save those I love. Maybe I could have saved Daison.

I haven't seen Kayla since I left Stonehill, and I wonder if Fen was right about her not being angry. I have my doubts, and they grow bigger the longer I go without a visit from her. I must remind myself we are at war with the Fae, under attack by the Druids. It's selfish of me to think that visiting would be Kayla's highest priority.

Three times a week, I return to the Crystal Palace as promised for my training with Varis. Most of the time we focus less on magic and more on history of the Fae, their customs and cultures. As the Druid works with me, Zyra trains Yami, and now my little dragon can fly for quite some time before he must rest on my shoulder. We are both growing stronger.

But today is different. Today, Varis forgoes our beginning meditation. Today, he hands me a warm cloak. "We must travel."

"Where?" I ask, wrapping it over my shoulder.

"To the Earth Tribe."

His words fill me with excitement. I've been to the Air Tribe, but not any other.

We leave the cavern and step onto the cold, snowy mountain. I turn to head up the steps towards the gryphon, but Varis does not follow. Instead, he whispers to Zyra, and the silver owl flies high into the sky, disappearing into the glare of the sun. When she descends, she is giant, larger than a gryphon, magnificent and fierce, her long talons and feathers gleaming in the light.

She lands before us, and the gust of wind from her wings nearly knocks me off my feet. Yami can't contain himself. He jumps off my shoulders and flies over to her, his wings a flutter of flurry and excitement.

"This is another form of Zyra," Varis explains. "Yami, you too have many forms that you will someday uncover."

Yami lifts his head higher and preens himself, pleased by the idea that he will grow big and mighty too.

"We're to ride her?" I ask. Varis nods, and a thought occurs to me. "Does that mean I will someday be able to ride Yami?"

Varis smiles. "Someday."

"I'm going to ride a dragon?" I jump up and down like a kid.

Varis chuckles. "Get on the owl, Arianna. Time for silliness later."

I try to contain my smile, and he helps me onto Zyra. Riding a giant owl with no harness is about as uncomfortable and hard as one might imagine. I wrap my arms around Varis and hold on tight, as instructed. Yami wraps around my arm and together we take off into the sky.

I yell with joy.

Flying on Zyra is different than flying on a gryphon.

I don't feel like a passenger.

I feel like the wind.

I become the air. I am the flight. The bird and I are one, and I feel bliss flow through me.

Time seems to stand still, and I do not know how long it takes us to reach the Earth Tribe. We land on a natural bridge that stretches over a canyon. A waterfall falls before us. Giant rocks jut out from the ground, covered in green moss. Vines of red flowers crawl up the stone. More bridges run through the canyon below.

We dismount, and Zyra ruffles her feathers, and they burst into a great gust of wind. The spirit is small once again and perches on Varis' arm.

I shake my head, amazed at this ability, trying to imagine Yami being able to do something similar. I can't wait for our magic to grow more powerful.

A group of Fae approach, led by a woman dressed in brown furs, wearing bones as jewelry. Their skin is copper, not as dark as the Water Tribe, but darker than mine. They fall to their knees before Varis and tap their fingers to their chest, a sign of respect to the Spirits— something I learned in my lessons.

"Druid of the Winds, what brings you to our lands?" the woman asks.

"Rita, I have come seeking Lianna and her spirit, Tauren. They have not shown themselves at the Crystal Palace."

Rita, the leader, looks to the woman on her right in concern, then back at Varis. "The spirit has not returned to the Palace, because Tauren never awoke."

...

Rita guides Varis down the path of the canyon, and I follow. The Earth Fae do not give me their attention, and I wonder if they know I am the Midnight Star. Perhaps they do, and that is why they ignore me.

The path grows more and more narrow along the side of the mountain, and I fear falling off, but I do not voice my concern. This doesn't seem the time to be worried about heights. Or death.

We arrive at the base of the waterfall. It is a small stream, more elegant than the waterfalls in Stonehill, and we walk around the torrent and into a small cavern. An old tree grows there, its vines climbing up the brown wet stone.

"You see," Rita says. "Tauren yet slumbers."

Varis walks up to the roots and lays his hands on them. He puts his ear against the wood and closes his eyes, stilling his breathing.

I know what he's doing and I do the same, practicing the techniques he's been teaching me. I quiet my mind and focus on my breathing to see if I can hear what he's listening for.

"Girl," Rita says, pointing at me and breaking my concentration. "You are the one they call the Midnight Star?"

I turn to face her. "Yes."

"You are false," she says, spitting at the ground in front of me. "Your blood did not awaken our spirit. He still waits for Yami."

I straighten my spine and glare at the woman. "Yami is with me." I say. The dragon stands and stretches on my shoulder, in response to his name.

"Then show me," she challenges.

I look at Yami, and he shakes his head and cowers behind my hair, scared of the woman and her cruel speech. My face hardens. "You have been disrespectful to me and to him. We will do nothing for you."

I walk to Varis, leaving her standing in shock, her jaw hanging open.

Varis stands and turns to us. "By the Spirits..."

He frowns. Something is very wrong.

"Does Tauren still slumber?" I ask.

"No," he says, his eyes scared for the first time since I've known him. "He does not slumber. He was never here at all."

10

A FRIEND

"No need to throw yourself at me just yet. We'll
have our time together soon enough."

—Asher

I return to Sky Castle and turn my attention to the
Healing Tent. We no longer just treat those injured in the
attack, but anyone with ailments. My Druid training is
suspended for a few days, while Varis searches for Lianna
and Tauren, so I keep busy here. Seri begins to use my help
more and more often. Sometimes, she asks me to diagnose
a patient. I am often wrong. But a few times I am right.

"You are improving, Your Grace," Seri says.

"Please, call me Ari."

"Ari, pass the water basin."

I do, and she cleans her hands, sighing. The moon
is out, and it has been a hard day of work. Shadows loom
under her eyes.

"You are very skilled in this," I say. "Seems you are more use here than being Keeper."

She laughs. "Thank you. All my life, I've trained to be a healer. You may not know, because I am Fae, but I am young. Around your age. My grandfather was Keeper, and my older sister trained under him. I did as I wished, and I wished to heal people. I lost my parents to disease, you see. So I practiced with the healers. About a month ago, my sister was wounded, an attack in Stonehill. She died, and all my healing could not help her. My grandfather could not handle the grief. A few days later he too passed. I was the only one left in my family, and so the duty of Keeper fell to me."

I touch her hand. "I'm sorry. I too lost someone in the attack."

She looks up, surprised. "We are complicated people, are we not, Princess? The vampires keep me slave. But the Fae killed my blood. Sometimes, I do not know who is right. Sometimes, I do not know where I stand."

We both share the same struggle. Torn between two worlds. "We will find our way," I say. "*Dum spiro spero*."

She blinks. "What does that mean?"

"While I breathe, I hope."

She nods, a new certainty on her face. "Yes. You're right, Princess. *Dum spiro spero*."

...

The next day, while eating breakfast, Asher informs me it is time to visit Earth. I beam with excitement. I miss my friends, and Es would have just had her gender reassignment surgery. She'll want my support.

But there's another reason I'm excited, and it has nothing to do with visiting Oregon. In order to get to my world, we have to travel through Fen's realm, to the mirror on the outskirts. Which means I get to see him again. It's been weeks, and my longing for him has only deepened.

I'm practically bursting with joy as we step onto Asher's boat to sail north on the winding canals. The sun is high. The breeze warm.

Asher frowns at me. "Excited to see someone, are we?"

I blush. "Well... Wait. Are you... Are you jealous? I know this is your month with me, and we haven't had much time together to... bond."

He chuckles. "No. I'm not jealous. That would be Levi's department, not mine. I just hope you make this choice with your head and not your heart. Nothing good comes from making decisions out of emotion, trust me."

I lay down on pillows, watching the land change before me. "Does this have anything to do with Varis? How you used to be friends?"

He looks away. "It's just a fact. Be smart. Be logical."

I sigh, rolling my eyes. But inside, his words tear at me. I must choose the next king of hell. I must choose, not only for myself, but for an entire kingdom. What if the best ruler is not the one I love?

The air grows cold, and we arrive in Fen's realm. His castle looms in the distance, a giant mass of stone carved into a snow-covered mountain. Baron stands on the shore, awaiting our arrival.

When we step on land, he growls at Asher, then wags his tail and licks my hand.

The Prince of Pride scowls. "Nasty beast."

I smack him in the arm. "Don't be cruel. He's the best wolf in the whole world, aren't you boy?"

Baron grins, licking Yami. The dragon flies on his back and rides the wolf all the way into the city.

"I've got some business in town, so I'll trust you can find your way," Asher says.

I nod. "Meet you in a bit."

As I walk through Stonehill, I run my hands over the crystals dripping from stone and trees. Burned buildings mark the landscape. In the distance, a great scar covers the land where a forest once stood. Villagers greet me with smiles and bows and soon word spreads that the princess is back. I smile and speak to everyone I can, but when I see Kayla, I stop. My heart skips.

I don't know how she'll respond to me. We haven't seen each other since the night Daison died.

She jogs up to me and pulls me into her arms like a sister, and I nearly collapse from relief.

I sniff and wipe away a tear as she releases me. "I thought you'd hate me," I say.

"Never," she says. "We all make our choices. He made his, I made mine. If I had gone with you, many others would have died."

That's no easy comfort, but still, it eases something in me. "I'm so sorry, Kayla."

She takes my hand and leads me through the village to the memorial where so many were buried or burned. Daison wasn't buried, but a sword sticks in the ground under his favorite tree to commemorate his life. It is engraved with his name and the dates of his birth and death. I drop to the ground before it and water the earth with my tears.

Kayla joins me, and some time passes before we stand again, but when we do it is with lighter hearts.

"Thank you," I say to her after a time, as we head to the castle.

"No need. We did nothing wrong. The Fae brought this grief. And soon, we will have our revenge."

I feel a lump in my chest at her words, and I don't respond. How do I tell her that I am Fae, that I know their ways now? That I can't kill them anymore than I can kill vampires?

We pass Kayla's forge, where I made Spero with her assistance. "I could use some help," Kayla says. "You should come by later."

"I can't," I say. "But thank you."

She cocks her head, frowning. Can she tell I'm too afraid to pick up a hammer since Daison's death? That just being here, with memories of him everywhere, makes me itch?

A deep voice comes from behind me. "Glad I decided to come by," says Fen.

I turn and run into his arms.

Our embrace lingers for as long as I can allow. When I pull away, he is reluctant to let me go. "I don't have long," I say. "Asher is handling some business, then we are going to my world to visit Es. She's having her surgery."

Fen nods. "Wish her well for me. I liked her."

I smile up at me. "She liked you too."

Kayla walks up to us. "What brings you here, brother?"

"Preparations. How are the weapons?"

"Nearly done."

A girl with green hair walks out of the forge, carrying some tools that look recently cleaned. I recognize her. One of the Fae slaves I purchased to keep them away from Levi. She sees me and curtseys, her eyes guarded and cautious. "Min, this is Princess Arianna," Kayla says. "She was the one who—"

"I remember. She owns me," Min says with a challenge.

I smile. "That's true, but it is not the way I want it to be."

She snorts. "Words spoken by a slave owner."

Kayla sends her out for wood and apologizes to us. "She's sharp around the edges, but a hard worker with real talent for this. The rest of the slaves you purchased are also doing good work, have good homes."

"No need to apologize," I say, though I can tell Fen feels differently. I place a cautionary hand on his arm. "Min's been through a lot, no doubt. And she is still owned by another person, even if she's doing work she finds rewarding. I'd feel the same as her." I look up at Fen, with a firm expression on my face. "Wouldn't you feel the same in her position?" I ask, forcing empathy into his stubborn heart.

He grunts. "Very likely. Maybe."

Kayla laughs. "It's so good to see you here again, Ari. You're the only one who can penetrate his thick skull with sense."

I smile, looping my arm into Fen's. "Then I'll have to come around more often."

Kayla looks between the two of us. "There's something I need to tell you. Both of you. I'm going north with Salzar, to strike back at the Fae."

I squeeze Fen's arm. "I don't understand."

He sighs. "Salzar, one of my nobles, has been gathering a force to raid the Outlands. Many want vengeance for their lost families." He side-eyes Kayla. "And I am not one to deny them."

The Shade nods. "Thank you, Fen. I will have your order done before I leave. And Ari, I'm sorry I did not visit you in the Realm of Pride. There has been much work to do, but I hope to see you again soon. Now, go enjoy your time together." She kisses me on the cheek, then shoos us away and disappears into the forge.

I hold Fen's arm as we walk to the castle, Baron at my heel, Yami on the wolf's back. "You do not seem to support Salzar," I say.

Fen pinches his nose. "He has been a problem. I imprisoned him for a few days, hoping it would soothe his temper. But it only sharpened his rage. He stirred up a mob, gathered volunteers to raid the Outlands. I considered stopping him, but those people, the ones who would rather follow him than me, they are not the people I need in my realm right now. So I allowed one person per family to join Salzar. Let them raid. Let them satisfy their hatred. In the end, it helps us both."

I nod, understanding the sad logic. "What of you? How are you doing?" I ask.

"It has been difficult, balancing the demands of war with the need to rebuild and provide for my people."

I place my free hand on his shoulder. "You're a good man, Fen. You'll make the right choices."

He looks down at me, a guarded expression on his face. "You would not think so if you knew all."

"I know more than you think, and I still believe you are good at heart. Even good people make poor choices from time to time."

He freezes, staring at me. "Arianna, what do you speak of?"

"I..." There's so much I can't say, so I will him to say it for me.

He faces me, holding both of my hands in his. "I didn't know who you were until I woke having tasted your blood. Please believe me."

I sag in relief at his words. More than anything, I had to know: had he lied to me?

But I couldn't ask. The contract wouldn't allow it. Even now, I feel us skirting too close to the topic. I smile and squeeze his hands. "Thank you. That's all I need to know."

"So we are... good?" he asks uncertainly.

"Yes. We are good."

Asher calls my name and I turn, frowning. He's ready to leave.

Fen caresses my cheek. "Go. I will see you soon." He kisses me on the lips, gently. It's our first kiss since the cave, and I hold onto him, hold onto the moment where it's just him and me and no one else matters.

I can still feel the heat of his lips against mine as I travel with Asher past the wall, to the mirror, and enter my world once again.

...

We make fast time, heading straight to the hospital in Asher's limo. The moon is bright, and I roll down my window, enjoying the fresh cool air. Tall metal buildings pass us by, so foreign to me now. But Portland is less Sky Castle, more Stonehill, and full of comforting memories.

Asher looks at my neck and cocks his head. "Where did you get that fabulous dragon necklace?"

I look down and frown. Yami is wrapped around my throat like a collar, but he doesn't look real. He looks like jewelry. "It's Yami," I say.

"Ah, of course," says Asher. "Spirits are weaker away from their home world. He can't take living form here."

I tap Yami's head, wondering if he's dreaming. "See you soon, buddy," I whisper.

In moments, we arrive at the hospital and greet Pete in the waiting room. His red hair is wild, and dark circles hang under his eyes. I hug him and introduce him to Asher. "How is she?" I ask.

"She's out of surgery and recovering. I can't see her yet. But she's strong and doing well." I can tell he's nervous, but also happy she made it safely through.

"I'm sorry I couldn't be here earlier," I say.

"You're here now," he says, smiling. "That's what matters." He glances at my neck. "Nice necklace. I would almost swear it's—"

A doctor enters the room. "She's awake and would like to see you. Is there an Arianna here?"

I step forward. "I'm Ari."

"Es would like to see you as well."

I leave Asher in the lobby looking profoundly uncomfortable and follow the doctor to Es' room. She's hooked up to monitors and tubes, and she's far too pale, her blond hair a mess, but she's alive, and her smile is bright.

"Hey baby," Pete says, walking over to hold her hand and kiss her forehead. "You did great."

Her eyes are droopy from pain meds but she smiles. "I'm all woman now," she says.

"You have always been all woman," Pete says. "But I'm so glad your body feels more of a fit for you now. I love you no matter what. You know that, right?"

A tear leaks from the corner of her eye. "Yes, I know that."

"Hey, Es," I say, walking forward. "You're looking good."

She rolls her eyes and reaches for my hand. "Darlin', how I missed you. I need some makeup, and Pete, bless his heart, knows nothing about eyeliner. Now fetch my bag over there."

I get her purse and pull out her makeup kit, and for the next twenty minutes we talk as I 'do her face.' When I'm done, she examines herself in the mirror and smiles. "That's more like it. Now tell me, is that sexy hunk of yours here with you?"

"No, Fen had some business to take care of."

Pete wrinkles his nose. "She brought the other one. Asher."

Es raises an eyebrow. "That tall sexy suit? He's not too bad either. But I've a feeling you are all about Fen these days, aren't you?"

I grin. "I do like him a lot."

Pete frowns. "I wish I could have met him. This one… I'm not so sure about. Be careful with him." He is more right than he knows.

"Asher wouldn't hurt me," I say. And I believe it.

"If Pete is worried, don't take it lightly," Es says, then yawns. "Oh lordy, my meds are kicking in, kids. I don't think I'll be able to stay awake much longer." She looks at me. "Keep Pete company a bit, will ya?"

"I will," I say.

I leave them to say their goodbyes and find Asher waiting in the lobby.

"Can we please return home now?" he begs.

"I get half a day, remember?"

Asher rolls his eyes. "Of course. Maybe my father was right about me being too much of a pushover."

I grin at him. "Too late. No changing a contract made with former law students."

He rolls his eyes at me and I grin wider.

When Pete returns from Es' room, I tell them I'd like to visit my mother before we leave. She's in a different ward on a different floor, and Pete and Asher wait in the hall while I go in.

Her room is small but private, and she looks much the same as she did before. It's dark, the curtains drawn, the lights dimmed to give her rest. But her room smells pleasant, and I notice that in addition to the roses Fen has been sending her, there are vases of purple orchids in various states of bloom.

They were always her favorite.

I check the vase for a card, but there isn't one. I sit near her and hold her hand. How do I even begin to tell her what I've been through and what I'm still going through? I wish she was here right now. Awake. Alive. I wish I could ask her advice and listen as she makes the complicated seem so much simpler with her mom logic.

These are such selfish reasons to want her back, but she's my mom, and though I am an adult, I still need her.

I know she can't hear me, that she'll never be able to answer, but I spill my heart, and it lightens something inside me.

I'm telling her about Yami when the door opens. I stop speaking as a man comes in. He is tall, pale, with curly hair, a wild black beard and a scar across his face. He holds a bouquet of purple orchids.

"I'm sorry," he says, stepping back. "I didn't realize anyone was here."

I stand to face him. "It's fine. I was just visiting my mother."

His eyes widen. "You're her daughter?"

"Yes."

"Of course," he says. "I see the resemblance."

The comment strikes me as odd, since I look more like my father and nothing like my mother.

"We're old friends," he says. "Your mother and I."

"Would I know your name?"

He shakes his head. "No, probably not."

I tilt my head, studying him. He seems familiar. "Thank you for visiting her. I've been busy with work and haven't been able to come as often as I'd like."

"Your mother would want you out there, living your life. She always put you first."

Maybe he did know my mother after all. Because he's right. My mother did always put me first. She even traded her soul to save me, and what did I do? Give it all back to save her. Did I do the right thing, making that deal? Would she be sad or angry, knowing I signed my soul away for her?

The man holds up the flowers. "I brought these for her, but I think you might need them more tonight." He hands me the bouquet, and I study them, closing my eyes to breathe in the sweet scent.

"Thank you." I open my eyes to speak to the man, but he is gone. Vanished as if he'd never been there.

I could easily believe I imagined the whole thing, if not for the flowers. But why did he seem so familiar? Something about the kindness of his smile... and the green of his eyes.

...

Asher and Pete are waiting for me after I say goodbye to my mother, but neither saw the man I describe to them. Asher eyes my flowers. "He gave you those?

I nod.

"Curious," he says.

But the mystery is put on hold as we head back to my old apartment, now Pete's and Es' home. I'm impressed by what they've done with the place. The heater is working again, and they've decorated with beautiful art, tapestries and throw carpets, turning the living room into a colorful cozy nook, the walls lined with packed bookshelves. "I love it," I say, as I sink into my couch, now covered by a purple throw blanket.

Pete smiles. "It was mostly Es. She loves color."

Asher takes a seat next to me, admiring the purple.

Pete sits across from us. "I've been checking on your mom regularly. As you saw, she's doing the same."

I swallow a lump in my throat. With the war, with my training, with everything going on, it's easy to forget why I'm doing this. It's all been for her. "Thank you. I can't tell you how much that means to me."

Asher throws an arm behind me and crosses a leg over one knee. "So, Pete, Arianna here tells me you read fortunes."

"Yes," he says simply.

"Do mine, won't you? I'm dying to know my future."

I elbow him in the ribs. "Don't be an ass," I hiss under my breath.

He looks offended. "What? I genuinely want to know. Can't fault a man for wanting a heads-up about what's to be, can you?"

I roll my eyes at him, but Pete is already pulling out his Tarot cards. He asks Asher to draw three cards. "For your past, your present and your future."

Asher does, and Pete lays out the past. The Ten of Pentacles. On the card, an old wise man sits comfortably on a chair, surrounded by his family. Pete studies it. "You have lived a long life, accomplished much."

Asher raises an eyebrow and leans forward, taking this much more seriously now.

Pete turns over the second card. A man and woman embrace. The Lovers. "You're suspended between two possible courses of action. Both have their risks. However, you must choose one. Indecision will only make things worse."

"Well, that's just lovely, isn't it?" Asher says.

I shush him as Pete lays out the last card. A tower struck by lightning. His eyes widen. "The Tower. You will soon face disaster. Your previous preconceptions will be washed away, but in their place you will find new truth."

Asher looks uneasy. He adjusts his collar and checks his watch. "Time to catch a plane," he says, standing and leaving Pete and me to say our goodbyes.

I hug my friend. "Take care of Es. Take care of each other."

He nods. "Take care of you," he says. He pulls away and stares at me. "There's something different about you, Ari. Are you okay?"

I almost laugh at how true his words are. "People change, Pete. Life changes us."

"Just don't lose who you are inside."

...

Asher wants to go back to the mansion and head home, but I still have some darkness with which to play, and so I make him walk with me. "It's time you see how the 99% lives," I say, dragging him down the street. A light rain sprinkles from above. Cars hum and a dog barks in the distance.

"I do not want to see how the 99% lives, thank you very much. I'd much prefer staying in my 1% of the world, whichever world I happen to be occupying."

I shake my head. "You're going to walk with me, and we'll talk and get a drink and for another few hours I'll get to be the girl I used to be before all this happened."

"Very well, Princess. If you insist."

I link my arm through his and we walk. I show him my favorite knick-knack shop, and the place I like to go for coffee. Everything is closed, of course, so we head to a bar instead, and I order us the frilliest drinks on the menu—mine's a virgin of course. Since I am clearly not the law in this world. His has an umbrella and several cherries.

We sit outside, watching mostly intoxicated people pass us on their way home from the bars.

"You know, I must admit to a bit of envy," he says suddenly, as I sip my drink.

"Of what?"

"Of you. Your friendships. Es and Pete, they're family to you."

"They are," I admit.

"It must be nice, having people mean something. To me, everyone is a piece on a board to be manipulated."

We finish our drinks and continue our walk. The weather is turning cold, and I pull my jacket closer to me. I miss the weight of my sword on my hip, but love that I get to wear jeans here.

"That's a sad way to live," I say as we walk across the street and through a park. Couples stroll together in the distance. Ducks swim through a pond, hunting for any treats left by picnickers.

We stop near the water, watching the birds.

"I suppose I learned it from my father," Asher says. "I never really thought to question it, but you have a way of making me view my life differently."

I turn to look at him. At his blue eyes and chiseled face. "Surely not everyone is a pawn in your game?"

He raises his hand to my cheek. "Not everyone."

He's not Fen. But he's Asher. Handsome, debonair, charming Asher. Someone who believes in peace, who's fighting to make that dream a reality. He might be the best choice for king. Don't I owe it to that world to see if there's a spark?

And so when he asks if he can kiss me, I nod.

Our lips come together.

And it is tender. And sweet.

And like kissing my brother.

That is, if I had a brother.

We pull away from each other.

He looks at me oddly. "Nothing?"

I shake my head. "Not really. No offense."

"None taken. It was... odd."

I laugh. "Thanks."

"You know what I mean," he says, nudging my shoulder with his.

"I do. The problem is, I don't think I'm the one you should be kissing."

He says nothing, but I know I'm right by the faraway look in his eyes. "There are many ways these things can work out," he says.

"Really? Like what?"

He turns to me and smiles in his most charming way. "Marry me. I will not insist on fidelity. You can have Fen and still be queen. Choose a king who will be best suited to rule our world."

I choke out a laugh. "So you propose to share me with Fen? Have you ever met your brother?"

Asher rubs his jaw. "You're right. That might not work out so well in reality as in theory."

"We are friends, Asher. Good friends. True friends."

"No… You're just saying—"

"No, Asher. I am being honest. So you see, the Prince of Pride does in fact have a friend."

His eyes gleam. A touch of tears. But only for a moment. He wipes his face and smiles. "But you still must choose a prince to marry and make king. And Fen does not wish to rule."

"But those choices don't have to be made tonight," I say.

"True, but they do have to be made."

"If there's anything I've learned over the last few months, it's that the future is impossible to predict. You never know what will happen to change the circumstances."

He sighs. "That may very well be, but contracts with demons cannot be broken."

I smile and pull my coat around me. "I know."

"Then why are you smiling?"

"Because if there's anything else I've learned, it's that every contract has a loophole. Even a demonic one. And I'm going to find it."

11

IN ITS WAKE

"It is loud, all consuming, layered like a chorus. It is soft and hard at the same time. It is gentle and furious. Not female or male. Something else. It surrounds me. It embraces and engulfs me."

—Arianna Spero

When we arrive back at Asher's castle, Seri is pacing in the front hall. The moment she sees us she runs over, straightening her silver dress. "There have been more attacks," she says. She sounds more confident since our last talk. "Wadu destroyed one of Zeb's trading ships, and Riku set fire to Niam's palace. The princes are meeting at High Castle to vote on a course of action."

Asher frowns. "When?"

"Now, my lord."

"Bloody hell. They'd better not make any decisions without me."

"Without us," I correct.

He sighs. "I suppose you better come along. After all, you're safest with a prince."

We leave the castle and step, once again, onto Asher's boat. The sun is high in the sky as we travel south. "We can't let them invade the Outlands," I say, weakly. I've been up all night, and it's taking its toll.

Asher nods. "I agree. If we head past the walls, the Druids will gather an army to meet us. It will be chaos. Both sides will suffer. And our hope of peace will be but a dream."

I fidget with my hands, thinking of alternatives. "Maybe we can offer a peace treaty."

He chuckles. "My brothers care not for peace, remember." Once again, I'm reminded why Asher would make the best king. "And if they capture one of the Druids... I pray they don't learn of the Waystones."

The stone doors. The elevators. The way into Avakiri. "Asher, how is it the vampires don't know of the doors?"

He stares out at the horizon. "When we invaded Inferna, we decimated all in our path. The Fae that could, began to flee. We thought they retreated to the Outlands. In truth, they fled to Avakiri. They sent armies back to meet us, to try and reclaim their lands. Every soldier of theirs was sworn to secrecy. They would die before revealing the purpose of the doors. When we slew the last of the High Fae on this world, we thought the war won. But then my father, through methods of torture I can hardly imagine, learned of the Waystones. He discovered the Fae still held half this world, still had armies, still had fortresses. He did not tell me or my brothers. He chose to have us believe we ruled all, had won all. In the end, he saved many lives."

I shake my head, confused by Lucian and what he told me in the cavern. Half his actions seem to breed war, the other half peace. "I understand how Lucian knew of the Waystones. But what about you?"

He looks away.

"Varis," I say, putting together the pieces. "You were friends. He told you of the doors."

He grins. "Perhaps my father told me recently?"

"No. You knew your way around the Crystal Palace. Around the Air Village. You had traveled those paths many times."

His smile grows wider. "Impressive, Princess. You know, sometimes I wonder if who you choose as king will matter at all. Sometimes I wonder if, in the end, you will rule us all."

White towers peek over the horizon. Banners of all colors flutter in the wind. High Castle.

We reach shore and make haste to the Council Chambers. They are dark, barely lit by blue torches. Grand chairs surround a round table. The banners of each prince hang behind their chairs. The brothers are already there, yelling at each other.

Asher clears his throat, quieting the room, and takes his seat before the purple eagle banner. I stand at his side.

Fen looks up and grins. Baron circumvents the table and greets Yami and me, and I pat the wolf's head.

Levi, his eyes tired, his white hair unkempt, points at me. "This is no place for the princess."

"She stays," Fen says, glaring at his brother.

Asher keeps his face emotionless. "I agree."

The princes exchange nervous glances. Ace checks the watch-gizmo on his wrist and shrugs. "She will be Queen one day. Let her witness the meeting," he says softly.

Dean scowls. "I don't see why she should be Queen of anything—"

"Enough already," Niam groans. "I vote the princess stays. Four against three. Now please, let us return to the matter at hand."

Zeb nods. "We should at least give the Druid's words serious consideration," he says calmly. "War will cost us all."

Dean scoffs. "Give serious consideration to freeing all the slaves? How would that work, exactly?"

Levi reclines in his chair, throwing his feet on the table. He runs his cold eyes across the room. "Yes, let's consider. How would it work? I suppose Dean would have to bathe himself again, and Ace would need to transport all the materials for his inventions by hand, and Zeb's nobles will need to pick their own crops. And Niam's lords—"

"Enough," says Niam. "Dean and Levi are right. From a financial point of view, this would never work. Our economy would collapse overnight. Our nobles, even the middle class, would revolt. We either fight the Fae or we fight our own kind. Seems a simple choice, to me."

"We fight the Fae," Levi says as spittle flies from his twisted mouth. "We defeated the Druids before, and we can do so again."

Zeb raises a finger in the air. "Technically, brother, we defeated the High Fae, and the Druids went into slumber. How could they have returned if the High Fae blood line was killed off centuries ago?"

My blood runs cold at their talk, and Fen looks at me, frowning.

"Someone must have survived," Levi says. "Which leaves us only one choice. We must find the High Fae and kill it, just as we did before. It will end this war before it even begins."

"I agree," Dean says. "Strike at the head and the beast will fall."

This is going too far. "What if there is another way?" I say.

Levi sneers at me. "You are not a part of this Council, girl."

Fen growls. "Let her speak."

Levi looks around for support, but Ace nods. "I too want to hear what the princess has to say."

I stand straighter, making sure to meet all their eyes at least once as I talk. "We don't know for sure the High Fae have returned, or who they might be. Maybe the Fae figured out another way of bringing the Druid's back. Instead of banking on a gamble, why not work with what you know."

"And what might that be?" Niam asks.

"You know the Fae want their people freed," I say. "That's not an unreasonable request. It's one you would be fighting for if the roles were reversed."

Levi attempts to interrupt, but Fen kicks him under the table.

I stifle a grin and continue. "What if, instead of releasing all the slaves, you turn them into paid workers instead? Give them a share of the profits, or maybe a share of the land. The economy could still function, with some tweaks, and the Fae would be free citizens. It might placate the Druids. It might be enough for a truce."

Niam taps the table with his finger. "And what if the Fae don't want to work for us once they are free? Do we force them?"

I don't have a chance to answer before Levi voices his objections. "Even if they do stay, how do we keep them in line? How do we keep them from using their magic against us?"

I clear my throat, gaining their attention. "Where I am from, there are many rules governing even free citizens. If we apply the same principles here, we can determine a few things: Citizens cannot leave their realms without very good reason and approval from their lord. They must pay for their own housing and food, so if they want to live, they must work. Fighting, or using magic without permission, is illegal, and will be punished by prison or worse."

Niam and Zeb raise their eyebrows, impressed. Have they not considered this before? These concepts seem so simple to me...

But then, I remember the curse. The curse that prevents them from learning things from Earth. The curse that keeps them stuck in their ways. And for the first time, I realize, I am not bound by such things, and this gives me power.

Dean frowns. "This won't work. You can't change a system that's been in place for centuries overnight without war."

Asher shrugs. "I don't see a better way. Given none of our options are optimal, let us vote on Ari's idea."

Levi scowls.

Niam nods. "Let us vote then." He glances at me, sympathy in his eyes. "The idea does have merit, Arianna, but it would cause upheaval. And if the Fae decide to invade despite what we do, we will be undone. I vote against freeing the slaves."

Dean leans forward. "The things slaves do in my realm, the pleasures and entertainment they provide… I find it hard imagining free men doing such things. I must vote against."

Levi nods. "I vote against as well."

Asher clears his throat. "Ari's plan could result in the least amount of bloodshed amongst our people. I give it my support."

Fen nods. "I am never one to shy from war, but I do not relish death if it can be avoided. I vote in favor of Ari's plan as well."

Zeb deliberates a moment, chewing on his lip. "If they will stay and work with us, for us, then I also vote in favor of freeing the slaves."

All eyes turn to Ace. His vote will determine the future. So much rests with what he is about to say. If we go to war, I might never be able to make peace with the Fae, and the slaves will never be freed. And if they follow Levi's idea of hunting the High Fae, my own life will be in peril.

I hold my breath and wait.

Ace sighs. "Perhaps, it is time the Fae were free. Perhaps—"

The castle trembles with a loud rumble. I grab the table, steadying myself. The brothers stand. Ace jumps up and turns to the windows behind him.

They burn with light.

The glass shatters. The wall tears open. And there, in the night sky, I see fire.

The phoenix.

Riku.

Everything happens in a heartbeat.

The spirit strikes with a flaming claw, smashing into Ace, sending him flying across the room. He hits the far wall with a deep thud, his burned flesh torn open across his chest and legs.

Sparks of fire catch on the wall banners, setting them ablaze.

I don't think. I just run to Ace, to help him, to pull him away from the fire now spreading in the room.

Fen yells at me to stop, but it's too late. The phoenix strikes again through the open wall, hitting a pillar in the center, causing the ceiling to fall around us. I jump forward, evading the falling rocks and scraping my knees hard on the stone floor.

The room is in shambles. A wall of debris separates Ace and me from the other princes. Fortunately, it has blocked the ruined wall as well, keeping the phoenix away. Through the stone, smoke and dust, I hear the spirit screech and the princes yell.

I worry for Fen, for Asher, for Baron, but I can't do anything to help them right now. Yami trembles on my shoulder as I inch closer to Ace. The fire has spread throughout the room, a raging inferno around us. "Ace, we have to get out of here before we choke on the smoke or burn alive."

His eyes open slowly, and he nods. "Help me stand," he says, his voice cracked and fading. His body is burned and bleeding. His flesh smells cooked. Images of Daison fill my mind. I push them away.

I lift his body as gently as I can, but the man is heavier than he looks, and has very little strength for standing on his own. I sag under his weight. As we stumble forward, I realize I will not be able to do this much longer.

"Yami, can you help?" I whisper, hoping Ace is too out of it to wonder why I'm talking to myself.

Yami jumps on my arm and breathes a burst of blue flame at my skin. It burns and I yelp, nearly dropping Ace, who groans from pain. I look back down at my arm and see a dark blue mark forming there, a tattoo, like the kind the Druids have. I whisper the incantation for illusion and it disappears from sight, but I feel the effects of the mark. My body is stronger, filled with new power. I lift Ace higher, and we move forward easier than before, entering a long hallway.

"How do we get out of here?" I ask.

"There's no way down to the exit from here. We must cross a bridge to the other half of the castle," he says. He points to the left, and I follow his directions until we reach a silver archway leading outside. A bridge spans the two sides of the castle, from one tower to another. It is dark, the stars are bright. The ground is far below. The wind is strong.

I look down, over the edge, shaking from fear and adrenaline. If we run into the phoenix, we will not make it across this bridge. But the skies look clear. Riku must be preoccupied with the other princes. I try not to think about what that means for Fen and Asher. I have to focus on helping Ace, who fades more and more with each step.

I mumble an incantation under my breath, hoping to turn us invisible. I look at Ace. He's not invisible, but translucent. So am I. By the Spirits, this is difficult. Well, at least we'll be harder to see from a distance.

I take a step forward, propping Ace up against my body as I do.

Another step.

A gust of wind almost knocks me over, but I keep my feet planted. Deep breaths. *One step at a time. One step at a time, Ari.* It's slow going, but we make it halfway across. Just a little more. Once we're down, I can find healers for Ace. I can save him.

"I see you, girl." A voice roars above. Oren. The Fire Druid.

I scan the skies. The phoenix erupts from behind a tower, circling us like prey. Oren's voice booms from within the spirit. "Leave the prince, and I will cause you no harm."

"No!"

"So be it."

The phoenix dives, and the ground trembles.

I fall to my knees, dropping Ace.

The spirit stands before me, huge, wreathed in flame. When it breathes, the very air burns with its breath.

The light from its wings turns night to day, blinding my eyes. But from within the shape of the bird I see the shadow of a man. Oren. He is there. Merged with his spirit.

His voice is low, powerful, reverberating through me. "Leave the prince, or you too will pay."

I stand, placing myself between Ace and the spirit, and raise my sword. I will fight. I do not know how I will win. But I will not abandon Ace, who speaks kindly, who thinks of freedom, to this creature of war.

The phoenix steps forward, shaking the bridge. "Very well, then." He raises a claw.

And then Yami makes a sound I've never heard before.

A roar so loud the winds seem to stop in its wake.

He leaps off my shoulder and into the air.

And he turns to dust.

Oren laughs within the phoenix. "Even Yami has abandoned you. Now, there is no reason for you to live, *Princess*." He spits the title like a slur.

My eyes burn with tears. I know I will die, and Ace as well. But I will not go down softly. I will fight. I will fight until I cannot lift my sword. Until I cannot open my eyes. I will fight until the end.

Dum spiro spero.

While I breathe, I hope.

And I still breathe.

Something catches my eye. Up above, amongst the stars, a giant shape emerges. I have seen it before. I have seen it in the Darkness.

It blasts down toward us.

It lands behind me like thunder. And the bridge nearly falls at the weight, tearing apart with cracks. I glimpse the beast at my back. Eyes like stars. Skin like midnight.

Yami.

The dragon roars.

And everything fades.

The heat.

The wind.

The fear.

There is nothing but that sound. Nothing but the Darkness.

The dragon charges. Over me. Straight into the phoenix. It tears into the bird's neck with its jaws. Oren howls in pain. And the two beasts fall off the bridge. They twist in the sky. Fire and darkness, ripping each other apart.

I whisper a prayer for my sweet, little Yami. *Please be okay. Please.*

And I lift Ace up and pull him across the bridge.

This side of the castle has not been touched by fire, and I ask Ace where we go next. He says nothing, and I realize he has gone unconscious. He's too pale, too listless. He's lost too much blood. I need to find him a place to rest.

I scramble through the halls until we reach what looks like the servant quarters. The kitchen is empty, and I lift Ace's body to the large table in the center and examine his wounds. They are bad, worse than I'd realized. I tear some of his clothes into pieces to form tourniquets for the still-bleeding wounds, then I look for a knife, and cut my wrist, allowing my blood to dribble into his mouth. I lift his head to help him swallow.

He chokes, then drinks. I let him feed until I feel dizzy and know I must stop before I pass out as well. I pull my hand away. The blood should help, but he has not awoken, so I do my best with the small amount of knowledge and supplies I have access to.

I search the kitchen for herbs and creams and find crushed lavender used for tea. Perfect. I turn the lavender into a salve as quickly as I can and rub it over his burns, then find another herb, Moonleaf, unique to this world, which will numb his wounds and put him to sleep.

I feed him the herb, and he stirs, opening his eyes. "I saw something, there, on the bridge," he says through fever. "Stars. Midnight. I have seen it before—"

"Shh... You're tired and weak. Seeing things," I whisper. There is fear in my voice. If he knows what I am, who I am, he will be a danger to me.

Ace's eyes clear for a moment, and he reaches for my hand, smiling. "Do not worry, Princess. I owe you my life. Besides, it is you who scares me... " His smile fades, and he falls into a restless sleep.

12

THE TRUTH

"One goblet contained poisoned wine. And how my father answered
my questions would determine which goblet he received."
—Fenris Vane

I use a bit of blood from my wrist to draw Fen's mark onto the floor. Hopefully, he will find us soon.

I wish I had a way to call Yami back to me as easily. I know he can't die as long as I live, but that doesn't mean he can't be hurt.

I close my eyes and try to meditate, try to reach out to Yami, but I'm too tired, sore and distracted to focus. Ace groans in his sleep, and I hurry to his side to check on him, but my medical skills are rudimentary at best. He needs a real healer, not a wanna be.

While I wait for the cavalry to arrive, I add wood to the hearth and stoke the fire back into life. We may have just nearly burned to death, but this room is cold.

Ace is still breathing erratically, and I consider giving him more of my blood when Fen walks in, looking crisp around the edges but very much alive.

"I felt the mark calling me," he says, pulling me into an embrace. He is bloody, burned, and covered in smoke, but I don't care. I pull away just enough to kiss him. He pauses, startled for a moment, and then his hands tighten around me, one dipping to my lower back and the other rising to the base of my neck to pull me closer.

He tastes of smoke and that woodsy flavor that is all Fen, and as the kiss deepens I lose myself in it.

It ends too soon. There are bigger things that demand our attention, but as the space between us grows and the heat of his lips leaves me, I miss it. I miss him.

"What happened after the room collapsed?" I ask.

"We fought off the phoenix," he says. "It flew behind the castle. Next time I saw it, it was falling through the sky, out of control. After a moment, it seemed to catch itself, then it flew away, one of its legs twisted."

I breathe a sigh of relief, glad Yami stayed invisible to everyone, glad he won the battle with Riku and Oren.

Fen drops my hand and walks over to Ace, studying his wounds.

"He needs healers," I say. "I gave him blood and did the best I could with what I know, but it isn't much."

Fen looks up. "Your blood?"

"No," I say sarcastically. "I gave him the blood I carry around in my purse for special occasions. Yes, my blood. What else?"

Fen shakes his head. "He'll know who you are now."

I nod. "He does, but he won't say anything. I trust him."

Fen raises an eyebrow. He begins to speak, when Seri arrives. She wears the tight silver dress Asher picked out, but her feet are bare. She left the shoes behind to make haste. A leather bag full of herbs and potions hangs from her hip, and she immediately sets to working on Ace.

A few moments later, the remaining princes barge into the room. They argue amongst themselves, about the slaves, about the phoenix, their gruff voices carrying throughout the kitchen. Fen whistles loudly to shut them up.

They don't.

But when they see Ace lying on the table looking near death, they quiet. Levi, in particular, looks grief stricken. He walks over to Ace and caresses his forehead. "How is he?"

The keeper looks up, a strand of blue hair falling into her eyes. "Not good. He is alive, but his wounds are great, even for a Fallen. Only time will tell. Right now, I need to get him to the Infirmary."

Levi leans down and whispers into Ace's ear so softly I cannot hear the words. Then he kisses his brother on the forehead and turns to the others. "We must not let this go unpunished."

Zeb, Niam, Dean, and even Fen nod in agreement. Asher looks cautious. "The plan to free the slaves is still a fine one," he says.

"No," Fen says, rage burning in his eyes. "We go to war. The time for peace has passed."

My heart drops. Fen knows who I am. How can he want to attack the Fae? But then I look down at the lifeless Ace. And I remember, the Prince of War will fight and die for those he loves.

...

Ace is transported to the Infirmary at High Castle and left in the care of Seri, while the rest of us regroup in the throne room: a giant hall of white stone, barren, and full of echoes. The brothers make a plan. All of us will travel north, stopping at each realm, gathering forces. When the vampires hear of what befell Prince Ace, they join the army eagerly. Those who hesitate still owe allegiance to their lords. Our numbers grow. Hundreds. Thousands. After three days, we arrive at Stonehill, the castle closest to the Outlands. The castle from where the princes of hell will wage war.

The entire time, Baron stays by my side and searches for Yami. As we sit in my Stonehill room, the fireplace crackling, he whines and sniffs at my hair, as if the dragon is hiding there. I pat his head. "I know, boy. I know."

It seems being away from Yami is tearing us both apart. Perhaps Varis will know where my dragon went. What if he returned to High Castle but couldn't find me? What if he returned to the Crystal Palace and waits for me alone? The thoughts and questions twirl around in my mind until I can't think straight.

I'm grateful for the distraction when someone knocks on my door. "Come in."

Fen enters, and my heart does a little flip. It's so strange, how just the sight of him makes my body sigh with happiness, even in midst of war and fear.

I try not to think about how we can't be together.

How my destiny and his are entirely opposite.

How he wants war when I want peace.

How he has no desire to be king, and I must be queen of this kingdom and that of the Fae.

Instead, I take a deep breath and smile and pat the rug next to me, and he sits, his long body folding into the space as he presses against my side.

I inhale his scent and enjoy the heat of his skin against my arm.

I stay in this one moment, where we are together and there is no blood or fighting or death. There is only us and a fire and a wolf and our feelings.

But these moments are made of dreams, and one must always wake.

"I cannot stay long," Fen says. "I must ready my troops for war. We march tomorrow at daybreak."

I lay my head on his shoulder, staring into the dancing flames. "Please don't fight. Please don't go to war against the Fae."

He kisses the top of my head. "I am sorry, Arianna. But the Council has decided, and I agree with that decision. The Druids nearly killed my brother, and he might die yet. They must pay for what they have done. They will not stop until we are destroyed, don't you see that?"

"It's not that black and white," I say. "Violence will only create more violence."

Fen shakes his head, and I raise mine, looking into his blue eyes.

"They killed Daison," he says. "Why do you care so much about peace with them? About their kind? I know you have their blood, but what does that mean? They kidnapped you. They killed the ones you love. They are not your people."

I open my mouth, prepared to tell him that not all Fae are as he imagines. That they have goodness in them.

Love. Kindness. That they are hurting and scared. That their world was destroyed and they are angry and they want their people freed. That not all Druids want war.

Agony grips me.

I fall from my chair, grabbing my throat. But still I do not give up. I need him to know, to understand. So I keep trying, through the pain, through the choking, until blood dribbles out of my mouth and I am coughing it up.

Fen catches me as my body convulses. "What it is, Arianna? What's happening?"

Baron whines and licks my face.

I try to tell him, and the pain worsens. My lungs burn. And so, finally, I stop trying.

The symptoms abate, leaving me exhausted and covered in sweat.

Fen's worried face flashes into something darker, more sinister, as the truth dawns. "Who?" he growls. "Who made you sign another contract?"

13

KARASI

Asher

"I'm glad you at least think I'm sexy."

—Asher

Everything has turned to a bloody mess and I, of course, must find a way to fix it before my plans go to rot.

Naturally that means sneaking back to Akaviri and trying to negotiate a truce. Now, how to keep my brother from waging war, that's a whole other beastly matter I'll have to sort out later.

But when I see Fen storming toward me, face-hardened by rage, I know I'll not escape the Realms unscathed by past sins.

His fist makes contact with my face, and I stumble back, rubbing my jaw. Why is he so much stronger than all of us, I wonder, not for the first time. "That will leave a mark, brother," I say. We stand in a cold, stone hall, the windows dark, the blue torches running low. The wolf is not here, fortunately. "But you needn't be so dramatic. It was just a friendly kiss. Nothing happened. You've captured her heart well and good."

Fen's eyes widen and his fist clenches again. "You *kissed her?*"

Well, hell. "I thought that's what this was about. No?"

"*Now* it is," Fen says, swinging again. At least he gave my other cheek a swing. Matching bruises and all. The symmetry is a nice touch.

"If this wasn't about the kiss, then what?"

"You made Ari sign another contract!"

"Right. That. How did you know?" I rub my jaw and stretch it out.

"She tried to tell me and it nearly killed her. I figured the rest out myself."

Strong girl, that one. Pity I can't muster up a good lust for her. We'd make a splendid couple, and fabulous rulers of this backward kingdom. But alas, she wasn't wrong in accusing me of pining for another. She wasn't entirely right, but she wasn't wrong.

Fen grabs my collar and lifts me in the air.

"Hang on now, you'll muss the clothing." I try to stay nonchalant, but the Prince of War is out for blood. My blood. It's hard not to take that seriously.

"I will kill you, Asher. What have you done to her and why?"

I've never seen Fen this angry. He raises a fist.

"It was our father!" I finally say.

That freezes him, and he drops me back to my feet. I use the pause to dust the wrinkles out of my lapel.

His eyes go wide. "Our father? But how? He's dead."

"He's not dead," I say. "He survived the poison. But he knew that what he wanted, what he planned, would never work the way things were, so he joined with the Fae and became allies, faking his own death in the process."

"He's been helping the Fae this whole time?" Fen steps back.

I nod. "He orchestrated the kidnapping of Arianna, organized the attack on you. I rescued her, but she had already signed a contract to not reveal his plans." A small lie, that.

"Why? Why didn't you tell me the truth, Asher? I trusted you."

I snort. "You trusted me? Really? Is that why you poisoned our father and then feigned shock when he died? Is that why you held a mock investigation into his death when you knew all along the one responsible?"

"You knew?"

I nod. "I saw you that night, leaving his room. I waited for you to tell me the truth, but you said nothing. So... why didn't I tell you? Because he was our father, and you hurt him. I saw how the thought of his death pained you, and I wanted you to feel that pain a little longer."

Fen clenches his jaw and fist simultaneously, his eyes burning with rage, and then all the anger seems to deflate. "It was never meant to kill him. That poison, it was only to subdue him while I tried to figure out his plans before he brought ruin to our kingdom."

"Don't you see, brother?" I look at Fen, the brother I've always loved more than the others. The one I trusted most until recently. "It's you who will bring ruin to our kingdom, if you persist in this war."

He says nothing.

I turn and walk away, leaving Fen alone to stew in his pain.

I don't have time to coddle the Prince of War.

When I'm sure I'm not being followed, I make my way through the snow-covered woods, running to save time, until I come upon the cave with the Waystone.

It's been activated with Fae blood, as per request, and I make fast time to the other side of the world, where Varis, Madrid and Durk wait in the dilapidated Crystal Palace. Lucian is there as well. Seems he returned from whatever business he had.

They sit around the dining table, drinking and talking when I arrive. I fill them in on what happened, and they frown.

"Then war has come," Varis says, his shoulders heavy. "We must consider siding with the Fae. If the Druids lose this battle, the Fae will never recover. It will mean the end of our kind."

My jaw hardens. "And if the princes lose, then *our* race will never recover!"

My father stands and slaps the table with his hand. "There is still a way to ensure peace."

How is it, again, that Lucian is now this force for peace? After so many years of bitter war, slavery and selfishness? Oh right, he never told me why.

He's still a gigantic ass.

"Maybe peace is a myth," I say. "A child's fantasy." I point at my father. "The Druids nearly killed your son. He's dying back in the Seven Realms as we sit here speaking of truce. How will my brothers ever forgive the Fae?"

Varis stands and paces the room. He raises a hand to his neck. Ah, a gesture I recognize. He is particularly stressed. His muscles bulge from pent up tension. "I will not support the demons in destroying the Fae," the Druid says. "I must protect my people above—"

"Above all!" I say, my voice too loud. "I have heard all this before. You speak of joining our two people, but always you side with your own."

Varis steps close and lays a hand on my arm, but I brush him off. Anger boils in me. I will not have this happen again. I will not be betrayed again.

Before I say or do something incredibly stupid, I push open the door and escape into the halls. I find a large balcony overlooking the mountains. The night breeze cools my hot face. I stare at the full moon and a sky full of stars. It's breathtaking, but not enough to distract me.

I know he's there before I feel his hand on my shoulder. "Asher... "

I turn on Varis. "No. I have something to say. Something I've kept inside me for centuries. And you will listen."

Varis, wisely, does not argue.

And the words suddenly get stuck in my throat. Standing here, in the moonlight, with him so real, so alive, so close. It's easy to forget the pain. The betrayal. But I won't. I can't. "How could you? How could you betray me all those years ago? Betray all of us? Our people? We had a plan. We would speak to my father and the Fae Queen. We would tell them our people could live in peace. That it could happen, because... " Emotion floods me, and I take Varis' hand, caressing it in mine. "Because it happened to us. We were going to show them our people could live together. Could love each other. Because we loved each other."

I turn away from him, dropping his hand, a tear threatening to escape my eye. "Was I wrong?"

"No," the Druid says softly. "You were not wrong, Asher."

I look up again, and see his eyes glistening in the moonlight. "Then why?" I ask. "Why were we attacked by your people when the meeting began? Why did you lead my family into a trap? My sister died that day, because of you."

His beautiful face contorts with grief. "Asher, I couldn't stop the High Queen. She learned of us, of our plans. She set the trap."

"Why didn't you warn me, Varis? Why did you let my sister die?" It has been years since I thought of Maya, since I let myself remember the girl who brought so much joy to a family full of men.

Varis looks away, ashamed. "I thought the Queen's plan would work, and... our plan? Of our people living together peacefully? I... didn't believe it then. Not truly. But... " He turns to face me again, his eyes earnest. "But I believe it now. I was wrong then. When I saw what happened to Maya, when I saw the hurt and betrayal in your eyes, I knew I had made a terrible mistake. I knew you'd never forgive me."

"Will you fight tomorrow? Against my family?" I ask him.

Varis doesn't avert his eyes this time. "Yes, but not to kill. I will fight to contain the war until the demons surrender. Then, I will end the battle. No lives will be sacrificed unnecessarily."

I nod. It's more than I could have hoped for, though not what I want. "I will do the same then. But we will be on different sides."

I turn to leave, but Varis reaches for my hand and pulls me toward him. He touches my face gently. "No matter what happens tomorrow, Asher, you are, and always will be, my Karasi. Spirit of my heart."

14

THE CHOICE

"This world cares nothing for me."
—Arianna Spero

Fire is everywhere. Filling my sight, lapping at my skin like hungry demons, burning my nostrils. Smoke clouds my vision, and I trip over a body. I'm scared to look down, because I know what I will see. What I always see.

Daison. He is stuck under the burning logs. He is dying. I pull and tug, but I can't save him. I can never save him.

His face morphs and now he is Ace, his chest caving in from talon scratches, his skin pale from blood loss, his body charred. I rip open my wrist and dribble blood into his mouth, but he does not awaken.

As I stare down in horror, his features change, and I am holding Fen. Fen, who is dying. Who is burned.

I cut open my other wrist. I bleed and bleed but I can never save him.

I can never save any of them, no matter how much blood I give.

...

My heart hammers in my chest, and I wake with a start, gasping in the cool, clean night air. I check my wrists. They are not slashed open. One is still bandaged, but it is healing. I am not dying.

But Daison is dead.

Ace might die.

And Fen.

Fen must live.

The wind shifts in my room, and I notice a silhouette in my window. A person. I slip out of bed and reach for Spero, holding my sword tightly in my hand as I walk over to the figure lurking in the dark.

"Metsi." I recognize her from the presenting, though I haven't seen her since. Her dark skins glows under the moonlight, and her serpent coils around her right wrist, placated for now. "Have you come to kill me in my sleep?"

"My brother, Oren, told me what you did, summoning the Midnight Star." Her voice is lilting, soft, Irish-sounding in its cadence, carrying on the wind.

My heart leaps. Does she know if Yami is okay?

"It is not too late," she says. "You can still side with your people. Fight with us, Princess. Fight with us and help us save the Fae."

I feel the pull of her plea, but I see in my mind what it would mean. I see Daison dead. Ace dying. I see Fen... bloody. "No," I say. "I cannot. I will not."

Her face hardens, and her serpent raises its head and hisses at me. Rain begins to fall outside. Lightning flashes. "Then you will fight for the demons? You will cause the annihilation of your people?"

"No," I say again. "Fighting isn't the answer. As long as both sides continue to seek blood for past sins, they will destroy each other. It will never end."

She cocks her bald head, her tribal tattoos catching the moonlight. "Right now, it is the only choice we have. You must choose, Princess Arianna. You must choose who you are. Are you the Midnight Star, sent to save your people? Or are you a pawn of the demons, aiding them in killing and enslaving our kind? Who will you be?"

Her words fade and her body turns to mist, disappearing into the night.

I walk back to my bed and sit on the edge, shaking from nerves, fear. I don't know what the right path is, but I'm sure all the ones that have been presented to me thus far are wrong.

The rain dies down. The lightning and thunder stop. I try to go back to sleep, but it will not come. I can't settle my mind or rest my body. I keep glancing at my window waiting for another visit, another attack.

So I pull on my robe and creep out of my room and down the hall to Fen's quarters. I knock, but he doesn't answer. When I open the door, the room is empty. Disappointed, I enter anyway and crawl into his bed. It smells like him, and for now, that will have to be enough.

...

I don't realize I fell asleep until his arms wrap around me.

I turn over to face him, placing my hands on his face. "Fen."

"Are you okay?" he asks. He pulls me closer to his chest, his arm wrapped around me, his large hand splayed against my back.

I love his eyes, love gazing deeply into them, getting lost in the piercing cobalt blue. "Is there anything you fear so much it keeps you awake at night?"

He closes his eyes, then opens them slowly. "Losing those I love." His arm flexes, tightening around me in a protective embrace.

My breathing turns shallow. "Fen... I... there's so much I want to tell you, but I can't."

He brings his thumb to my lips, caressing them. "I know. Asher told me. I know you were forced into another contract. I know my father is alive and behind all this."

But does he know about the Midnight Star? Does he know the plans they have for me? I can't ask him. But I'm glad this secret isn't a wall between us anymore.

"When I came to hell," I say, "I didn't expect it to be this... beautiful. Magical. I didn't think I would find friends. Family. Love." I hold my breath on that last word, waiting, but he just nods, encouraging me to continue.

"I feel torn between two worlds. And neither of them, bizarrely enough, are the world I was born in. But there's one thing I'm not torn about. Not anymore."

"What's that?" he asks softly, his breath caressing my face.

"My feelings for you."

"Ari..."

"No, let me finish. There's a lot I can't say, but I can say this. Fen, I don't know what our future holds. I don't know how this war will end, or who will become king, or even who *should* be king. I don't know what will happen with... " My throat constricts as I almost cross a line in talking about the Fae. I don't think we need to ruin another moment with one of us vomiting blood again. "With other things that shall not be named."

His lips twitch.

"But I know that even an immortal life is too short to ignore the heart. I know that I can't get you out of my head, and that the thought of anything happening to you nearly kills me. I know that I would give anything to keep you from going to war tomorrow, and not just because I'm worried about... things." I take a deep breath, but before I can finish my speech, Fen closes those few inches between us and kisses me. It's a gentle kiss. Soft. Warm. Tender.

"Ari," he says against my lips. "I love you. I have never cared for anyone as deeply or truly as I do you. And I cannot imagine losing you either."

Tears burn my eyes. I press into him, kissing him again. After a moment, I pull away to look into his eyes. "I love you too, Fenris Vane."

He strokes my face with his fingers. "I don't know what the future holds either, but we'll sort it out, somehow."

That night, I sleep in his arms, in the safety of our acknowledged feelings, however unknown our future is.

As morning breaks, something licks my chin. I open my eyes. "Baron?"

My baby dragon, now small again, peers at me with large dark eyes. "Yami!"

...

Fen and I linger in his room as long as we can that morning, and though he still cannot see Yami, I think he's starting to figure out Baron's odd behavior has a purpose. I, of course, can't tell him the truth yet, but I will be pushing Asher to end my contract as soon as possible. And I will not be signing another that involves secrets and physical pain.

"Would you like to join me in Stonehill today?" Fen asks as we head down to breakfast. "I must check on the soldiers before battle."

"I'd love to." I try to focus on being with Fen, and not on the war we are about to fight.

Asher is finishing up breakfast when we enter the dining hall with Baron at our feet. "There you two are," he says, dabbing his lips with a cloth napkin and standing. "Lazing about, are you?"

I snort and sit to eat. I find I'm famished after everything.

"Did you enjoy breakfast?" I ask Asher.

"Enough. But I'm in need of blood. Me and the other lads are getting restless." He turns to Fen, who sits across from me. "Where might we find a fresh source in your wild realm?"

Fen glares at him. "You know I restrict that sort of thing here, Asher. Make due with animals."

Asher grimaces. "How appalling. You live like such savages. How do you stand it, dear Ari?"

I shrug. "I don't drink blood."

He chuckles. "Not yet, at any rate."

Asher leaves before Fen gets any more angry, and I smile. "You two love each other. You should be kinder."

Fen looks up, narrowing his eyes. "He kissed you."

I nearly choke on my juice. "He told you?"

"Yes."

"Then he must have also told you it meant nothing. It was like kissing my brother, if I had a brother. Besides, I'm pretty sure I'm not his type."

Fen frowns. We eat quickly and walk to town. The army has set up camp outside the walls, since there isn't enough room inside. Baron trots between us, seeming quite happy that we are all together again. Yami rides on his back and occasionally flies over the wolf, causing Baron to bark and chase the baby dragon.

Fen just looks at me oddly, and I make a motion as if zipping my lips. He frowns, but doesn't push.

We walk to the outskirts of the city, to the largest crystal waterfall, the one that blocks the secret passage out of the Stonehill.

I rub the ring on my finger, the one Fen had designed for me. "I wear this all the time. It makes me think of this place. Of you."

We stand beside the water, crystals catching rays of sun, casting color and light everywhere.

"I don't need a ring to think of you," he says. He kisses me, and it's a lingering kiss. When he pulls away, I sigh. "I must check on the soldiers. We will leave soon."

"I worry for you. If anything were to happen... "

I touch his chest, and he covers my hands with his own. "I am the Prince of War. It is the Fae who should be worried."

15

WHAT IS IMPORTANT

Fenris Vane

"War is coming."

—Fenris Vane

I do not want to leave Ari, but Asher approaches, and I know it is to tell me that our brothers are ready and it is time to march. "I must go," I say quietly, touching the softness of her cheek.

"I know," she says. "But I wish you wouldn't."

I kiss her once. "My heart stays here with you."

"You are my Karasi," she says softly.

"Spirit of my heart," I say. I have heard the Fae speak of this, but have never felt it myself until now. Time will tell whether this love gives me strength or weakness.

Arianna nods. "You are mine. And I am yours. We are bound, you and I. Come what may, we are bound."

"I will leave Baron with you, to defend you," I say.

But Ari won't have it. "I'll feel better knowing he's protecting you. I'll be safe in the castle."

By the time Asher reaches us, we have said our goodbyes. Ari hugs Asher and whispers something to him I cannot hear, and then we leave.

"What did she tell you?" I ask my brother.

He looks at me with an odd expression. "She told me we find more strength in love than in hate."

I should not be surprised that somehow Arianna heard the words in my heart and answered them. It is not the first time she has done so. "She is wise. We do not deserve her."

Asher nods. "In that we agree."

A Shade boy runs up to us, breathless. "The Fae army has breached the great wall, they're gathering north, just near the Outlands," he reports.

Remembering Ari's kindness, I tell the boy to fetch some food and drink before heading back.

Asher grins at me. "She really has stolen your heart, hasn't she?"

I frown and walk faster.

The armies of the Seven Realms gather outside Stonehill, near the burned corpse of a forest, each stationed with their colors. Ace's soldiers are under my command, since he is still convalescing at High

Castle. Asher and I enter a grand red tent, large enough to fit dozens of men. Levi, Niam, Dean and Zeb wait inside, gathered around a war table full of maps.

Levi points to one. "Let us march forward, into the northern woods, and cut them off."

"No," I say. "We must avoid the forests. If they are set on fire we will burn alive within them. And we must stay far from the rivers unless we wish to battle Wadu once again."

"Where does that leave us then?" Dean asks, who at least came dressed appropriately for once in battle gear and armor.

"The mountains," I say.

Asher groans, but does not disagree.

Levi shakes his head. "They will slow us down, and if we are caught in the lower ground, we will be at a disadvantage."

"That will not happen," I say. "Not if the Druids think we're somewhere else."

Zeb nods. "What do you propose then?"

"A decoy," I say. "We send in a Shade we trust who claims to be a deserter. They tell the Druids we are taking the river pass, that we feared the forest because of fires, but we were less concerned with the Water Druid. We fought her off before."

"And why would they believe this person?" Levi asks.

"They are too caught up in the idea that all Fae and Shade are on their side, that no one with Fae blood would ever willingly fight for us," I say. "The Druids have slumbered for thousands of years. They do not realize things have changed. They do not realize there are Fae and Shade who would fight and die with us and not with them, even if given the choice."

Levi crosses his arms over his chest. "Let's say that's true. How can *we* trust the Shade not to betray us?"

"They won't know enough of our plan to give much away, so the risk is small."

"It's our best plan," Dean says, surprising me. "I agree with Fen."

Zeb, Niam and Asher all agree as well. Levi frowns, but doesn't argue. I call a Shade boy over and tell him what his orders are. He looks nervous, but I remind him his actions will help save Princess Arianna, and his eyes light up. He will do as I ask, that much I'm sure of.

Once the boy is off, my brothers and I send our scouts forward and take the lead at the head of our armies. We march up the mountains, against the snow and wind, to claim the high ground before the Fae take notice of us.

It's a long, hard hike, made harder still by the continuous deluge of rain pouring down like waterfalls. "It's the blasted Water Druid," Niam grumbles. "She's trying to drown us before we even have a battle."

Asher rings out his cloak, a look of distaste on his face. "It's working. I feel as if I might never be dry again."

"At least this will make our forests harder to burn," I remind them.

"I wish Ace were with us," Asher says. "He might have a nice invention to make this miserable climb a bit more pleasant."

At the mention of Ace, everyone's mood turns from frustration to grief. Levi seems to be most affected, patting Asher on the shoulder as he passes. "He will be with us again soon, brother," says the Prince of Envy, his red cloak wrapped around him.

It takes many hours to reach a plateau high enough and large enough to make camp. Our commanders report to each of us and rally the soldiers to their stations, setting up shifts for guards and patrols. We pick an area separate from the rest to bed down for the night.

By the time the moon is high in the sky, the rain finally stalls out, giving us a brief reprieve.

"Maybe she ran out of magic," Dean says, taking off his shirt—naturally. He grins as we all groan. "What?

It's soaked. I'm drying it. Don't be jealous of my majestic physique. We can't all be this irresistible."

Asher chuckles. "We can't all be that annoying either."

Zeb brings out a plate of cheeses and meats and two bottles of wine. He holds up one. "Alcohol." Then he holds up the other. "Blood." He places them both before us. "I have more. Choose your poison."

Most opt for both, mixing the blood and wine into a vampire cocktail. I take neither. I've had blood recently, and I don't wish to dull my senses with alcohol before battle. I advise my brothers to show restraint, but Zeb laughs.

"Eat, drink and be merry, Fen. Tomorrow might be the end," he quips.

"Yes, especially if you're hungover," I remind him, but he doesn't listen, not that I expected the Prince of Gluttony to stop drinking.

"How did you fit all this in your pack?" Niam asks, filling another glass.

Zeb smiles. "Magic."

It doesn't take long for the combination of blood and wine to make them all drunk and nostalgic. I poke at the fire with a stick and listen as they reminisce about a past so long ago it's almost a dream to me.

"Remember when we were kids, and Dean got lost in the Silver Gardens?" Zeb asks. He speaks of the Old

World, the time before the Fall. When we weren't the Fallen, but the Chosen.

"He claimed it wasn't his fault, that the place was huge," Niam says.

Asher chuckles. "He was too busy staring at his reflection in the statues to pay attention to where he was."

Zeb laughs. "And it was Levi who found him first, but then... " he laughs so hard he nearly chokes and takes another drink before continuing. "Then they both got lost."

They all chuckle at that, and Niam chimes in. "Then I got the rest of us together and made a plan. We'd go looking, but mark our way with coins."

"Great plan," Asher says, "only you were too greedy to use your own."

Niam nods. "True. I believe you covered that expense, Asher."

Zeb points to Levi and Dean. "And then remember, how we found you two, and it was so late, so cold, you two were cuddled up like lovers behind one of the statues?"

Dean shrugs and Levi shakes his head.

"But the best part," Zeb says between drinks, "the best part was when Ace jumped out of the shadows and landed next to us. He asks you where have you been all day, and you say 'stuck in the maze' and he says, 'well why didn't you just fly out?' Then the cheeky bastard hops into the sky and leaves us idiots behind."

Everyone laughs at that, but I frown. "Why don't I remember any of this?" I feel like I've heard the story before, but I have no memory at all of it happening.

My brothers look around at each other, and Zeb pats me on the shoulder. "You're getting old, good fellow. Soon that wolf of yours will have to run the kingdom." Baron whines and lays his head on my lap while the rest laugh.

As the fire begins to die down, so too do the laughs, and though we do not need much sleep, we each retreat to our own space, to think, to ponder, to plan for war.

...

The next morning, our scouts report they found the Fae army, hundreds of soldiers, camping behind one of the forests near the river. "This will be our best chance," I say. "We must strike early, while those awakening are still sluggish, and those on guard for the night are tired and ready for rest. It is when they change shifts that they will be most vulnerable. We travel down slowly, hiding behind the trees, and surprise them."

"We'll be close to the river," Asher says. "Do we not fear the Druid's powers so close to her element?"

"If we move fast enough, and with enough stealth, we'll win the fight before they can muster a counter attack," I say.

The five of them nod in agreement, and we choose the soldiers to head the first assault. The rest of the army will follow behind closely. We stay hidden behind stone and tree, moving silently through the forests, and down the mountain. We span out in a semicircle, some entering through the cover of river, so that we can take out their sentinels before they can react.

Step by step we move forward. All my senses are alert, searching for an ambush. Baron's ears point up, taking in all sounds, his teeth bared, ready to fight.

No one sees us.

No one raises a cry.

It's too quiet.

Too easy.

Something is wrong.

We descended on the camp, and I see the truth.

There are no Fae standing watch.

No Fae sleeping.

The camp is empty.

Levi dashes into a tent, his sword drawn, then comes out, a frown on his face. "There's no one," he shouts.

The others confirm the same.

And then I understand.

We thought we were so clever, going after them rather than letting them attack the castle.

But why would they be here? There is nothing important here.

Everything that is important to them, the thing that is most important to them... is at Stonehill.

16

BLOOD AND PAIN

"Long ago, Madrid and Oren, the Fire Druid you met
tonight, were Karasi—spirit of the heart. She has waited
for his return for many, many years. But Oren made her
choose: You—the Midnight Star—or him. She chose you."

—Durk

I pace my room while Yami flutters around me, mirroring my own anxiety. None of this feels right. The armies shouldn't have left to chase the Fae army. Stonehill is defensible. The Outlands are not.

The city and castle feel nearly abandoned with everyone gone. Even Kayla is off raiding. There's a knock at my door, and Julian enters with a tray of food and a mug with something steaming in it. "I thought you could use something to eat and a hot drink to stave off the chill."

She sets it down on my table and walks to the hearth to stoke the fire.

"Thank you," I say, picking at the grapes. Yami eyes the strips of ham, but I glare at him until he backs away from the food. He knows better than to eat when he's being invisible.

Julian stands once the fire is blazing again. "Can I get you anything else?"

"No, thank you though. Where's Kara?"

"She's helping Olga in the kitchen with dinner," Julian says.

"Okay, well, I'm good for the afternoon, so don't worry about me."

She leaves, and I feel a loneliness descend upon me, but I don't want company, not really.

I want Fen.

He shouldn't have left. Of that, I am more and more certain.

If I were the Fae... which, I guess, technically I am... I would just find somewhere safe to hunker down and wait for the battle. Maybe near water or the forest or a fort... or...

A castle.

I drop my grapes back onto the tray and run to the balcony outside my room, my eyes scanning the horizon. I can make out the village of Stonehill from here, and the mountain that connects it to the castle. The gate is sill closed, but there is another way in, the way behind the waterfall. Did the Fae learn of it during the attack on Stonehill?

I look more closely, my heart beating frantically in my chest. Shadows move behind the water.

They are coming.

The Fae army is coming, marching through the passage that was meant to be a safe haven for the village.

A burst of flame shoots through the sky, and Oren, the Fire Druid, appears before me, the phoenix in his hand. "You chose wrong, girl!"

Yami throws himself at the phoenix, attacking with teeth and claws, but the spirit bites him, pinning him down with sharp talons. Yami yells and turns to dust.

I draw my sword, Spero, and face the Druid. He draws his own blade, a thing of black steel wreathed in flame. I charge.

Our blades meet.

And Spero shatters. Breaks in half. The force of Oren's blow knocks me down to the ground, near the balcony's edge.

He walks up to me, his body in flames. "Now you are mine."

I can feel the heat emanating from him. It is my nightmares made real.

He chuckles. "The princes have lost. We have taken Stonehill, and soon we will destroy the demons. You should have sided with your people, when my sister gave you the chance. Perhaps she would proposition you even now, but I am not so forgiving." He holds his sword to my neck, burning my skin. "Your beast hurt my spirit. You owe me blood and pain, and I have come to collect."

17

WILL WE ALLOW IT
Fenris Vane

*"There is too much temptation to touch her, to hold
her, and having her so close but not quite close enough
is a sweet kind of torture I am unused to."*
—Fenris Vane

Our armies move slowly, so my brothers and I take
our best soldiers and run ahead, using all our speed and
strength to get back to Stonehill.

I feel the omen of death in my gut.

I made the worst mistake of my very long life, and
now the person I love most is in danger.

Baron howls as he runs. He knows Ari's in trouble.
He knows we have to reach her before they do.

But I know it's already too late.

By the time we arrive at Stonehill, green Fae banners hang from the walls. Fae soldiers guard the

perimeter. When we approach, they raise their spears and swords. But they do not attack.

"At last you have joined us," booms a voice atop the wall. A man. Huge and bulging with muscle. Red tattoos cover his bald head. Ash covers his hands. The Fire Druid. He's been waiting for me, and now that he has an audience, he performs.

He points his black sword to the figure beside him. A woman tied to a chair, her mouth stuffed with cloth. Ari.

"Let her go," I demand. "She is not what you came for."

The sword bursts into flames, and Ari screams through her gag. I can smell her flesh burning, and every muscle in my body tenses.

"Surrender!" The Druid's voice carries far and wide, full of rage and blame. "Surrender, or I will torture this pathetic creature."

"You won't kill her," I shout. "You need her." I realize I'm giving too much away. My brothers, most of them at any rate, don't know who she is, or why she's important. But I do. Asher does. I lean over to my brother and whisper in his ear. "She is High Fae. They can't hurt her, can they?"

"They won't kill her. It will send the Druid's back into slumber. But that doesn't mean he won't make her wish she was dead," Asher says, frowning.

I growl.

The Druid slices Ari's arm.

She screams.

Baron howls in misery.

I must decide. Arianna, or my people.

I will never sacrifice her.

But surrendering won't save anyone. The Fire Druid seems mad with power and vengeance. He will not release her, no matter what we do.

I leap up onto a boulder and shout to all who might hear. To the vampires held captive. To those soldiers on their way. To the Fae and Shade who have lived with us these many years. My voice carries throughout my realm. "These are the Fae who killed our families. Who took our homes. Who burned our crops and burned our forests. And now they have Princess Arianna. They torture her. This woman who has shown us all nothing but kindness. Who has fought for equality and justice for the vampires, Fae and Shade of our land. Who has helped all of you in one way or another. Will we allow them to hurt her? To torture her? To use her as a pawn in their games against us?"

The people roar. The armies roar. They are ready to fight. And we charge forward, bloodlust in our hearts.

We will save our princess.

18

MIDNIGHT STAR

*"He has more names than the others. One you
may have heard... the Midnight Star."*
—Madrid

Oren stands over me, gloating, his sword ablaze as he cuts into my arm again and again. I try not to cry out, but I can't hold it in.

The pain. The scent of my own burning flesh. My nightmares are made real. Both my arms are lined with the red ribbons of flame from his torture, and I can see in his eyes he takes pleasure from this. How did Madrid ever love this monster?

Another cut tears into me.

The pain consumes me. It is all I know or will ever know again. Pain. Burning.

I slump in the chair I'm tied to, the fight in me dying as my body weakens.

Oren speaks to the crowd gathering below. To the vampires. To Fen.

When I hear Fen's voice, something in me awakens once more.

I cannot give up.

I cannot let Fen surrender to this monster.

Fen delivers a speech, but I can't make out the words through the pain. Still, the cadence of his voice caresses me, bringing me a kind of peace in my darkness. And then the armies cheer. And I hear them charge.

Oren steps back, a look of shock on his face. It fades. "I should have known. The demons care for nothing—"

He is close enough now. I slam my head into his, and he falls back, stunned. I use the distraction to throw my body over the edge of the balcony.

I have no plan. No way of stopping the fall. I'm still stuck to a damn chair. But I refuse to be used as a pawn in their game. I refuse to be tortured more in order to control Fen.

I will die my own way.

I brace myself for the fall, for hitting the ground hard and—if not dying—at least breaking my bones. But honestly, what is a bit more pain at this point?

The ground rises up to greet me, and I close my yes, but then... I begin to slow down. How? Yami? I look around for my dragon, but he is not here. It's not a dragon catching me, but wind.

I land gently, and Varis lands beside me and helps me out of my restraints. "You will not be harmed," he says. He sees my arms and flinches. "I am sorry I did not arrive in time to stop him."

I try to thank him, but tears sting my eyes as another round of pain sweeps through me.

The air grows cold, and Metsi, the Water Druid, appears before us. Her serpent, Wadu, coils around her right arm, hissing. She raises a silver sword.

Varis raises his hand. "No, sister. The Midnight Star is not our enemy. We need her. She is the key to peace."

Metsi pauses, considering his words. She too notices my arms and frowns. "The vampires are nearing. They will be upon us soon. But it will be as you say, Varis. I hope you are right about her." She drops my broken sword at my feet and vanishes into mist.

"I must leave," Varis says. "Stay safe. When this battle is over, I will make sure both sides yet live."

With the air under him, and his owl at his side he rises into the sky, straight for the phoenix who flies above us.

I shake as I drop to my knees, the snow cool under my body. I pack it over my arms to soothe my burns. The cold is nearly as painful as the heat, but I know it must be done.

To manage the pain, I inhale deeply and exhale slowly, using meditation techniques Varis taught me. I must regain my focus and find Fen. He's in trouble. A deep knowing stirs within me. He's in danger, and I must help him.

I pick up my broken sword and whisper a cloaking illusion. Once again, I turn translucent instead of invisible. Still, it helps to stay hidden as I trudge through the snow, searching for Fen. Where would he be? I look up, following the traces of fire in the bright sky. It leads to Stonehill.

Soldiers clash around me. Steel rings in the air. The vampire army has arrived, and the Fae have left the city to meet them. The gate is open.

I jog faster, ignoring my pain, evading the fighting around me. As I turn past the gate, a Fae soldier sees through my illusion and lunges at me. I block his sword with what remains of mine. A vampire slides a spear into his back, and I nearly trip as I watch the man die.

This has to end.

The city burns. It is as before. Nothing has changed. For all I have done, there is no peace.

I run to the other side of the castle, to the clearing by its gates, where fires blaze the brightest. In the midst of the flames, upon charred black land, I find Fen and Baron in battle against Oren. His phoenix is above him, in the sky, fighting Zyra, twisting through the air. Varis rides his giant spirit, guiding her, striking at the phoenix with a blade. Below, Fen fights with speed, agility, and a deadly blade, but Oren is larger and stronger. His hands are alight with fire, and he throws flame at Baron.

Dead bodies litter the ground around them, some Fae, some vampire, some Shade. All wasted life.

Baron lunges at Oren.

The Druid raises his blade.

And cuts the wolf's paws.

Baron falls, whining. Fen roars, attacking with more ferocity than before. But the Druid matches every blow. He pushes Fen back.

The vampire is growing tired. Oren is too strong. He strikes. Again. Again. And Fen falls to his knees.

Fen can't win this fight alone.

I run forward, jumping between Fae and vampire. "Stop!"

Oren laughs. "Did the vampires stop when they were slaughtering my people? Did they stop when they murdered my Queen?"

"It is a cycle that never ends," I say, as the histories of these people spread out in my mind's eye. "The vampires were cast here against their will, cursed with blood lust, ravaged with this new desire, only to find a people whose blood was an addiction."

"Am I to feel pity for them?" Oren asks. "Am I to offer mercy to these monsters?"

"What they did was not right. The slavery isn't right. But there is another way. We can free the slaves," I say, grasping onto hope. "Turn them into workers. Look around you," I shout. "Too many lives are lost, and not just vampire, but Fae, Shade, your people!"

He throws flame at me, and I leap to the side, avoiding incineration. "What would Madrid want? What would she say to what you've become?"

Oren pauses. "It is... too late for us," he says softly. "It is too late for peace!" Oren rushes at me.

Fen dashes forward. He knocks me out of the way, putting himself in front of the druid. He strikes, taking Oren in the shoulder.

And Oren takes Fen in the gut.

The Prince of War falls, his body charred and bleeding. I collapse at his side, holding him, pulling him close. Baron stands beside us, whining, licking his master's face. I place my head on Fen's chest. He is barely breathing. His eyes won't open, and I can feel his life slipping away.

He's dying.

My love is dying.

My chest constricts.

I can't breathe.

Tears fall onto his ravaged face. "Fen, please. Be strong. Stay with them." This is my fault. This is all my fault. He will die because of me. Because I brought the Druids back. Because I changed the fates.

Oren looms over us. He rends Fen's blade free of his shoulder and throws it aside. No.

Not my fault.

Let's put the blame where it belongs, shall we?

I hate to leave him, to move apart from him, but I must. I lay Fen gently on the ground and kiss his forehead. Then I stand, my broken sword in hand, my tears drying and my grief turning to wrath.

"How can you do this?" I ask, my voice icy cold. Deadly. "How can you destroy so much life?" Words form in my throat that are not mine alone. Something else speaks through me. "This is not why you were chosen." I step forward, all fear gone. All weakness and pain gone. "This is not your duty." I hold my sword up and point it at the Druid as all my illusions fall and I reveal myself as Fae. "You have failed your people. You have failed yourself. You…"

Oren stumbles back.

"Are…"

He falls to his knees.

"Not…"

His fire fades.

"Worthy."

"No!" Oren pleads, fear in his eyes. His phoenix fizzles in the sky, turning to ash. "You will not take Riku from me. You will not... "

"The Wild Ones, the Spirits of our people, they belong to no one." I slash my sword through the air, and where once it was broken metal, now it reforms with the colors of midnight. The blade strikes the Druid through the throat, and he collapses, his life bleeding out of him. His eyes lose focus, fading into the afterlife, and a golden red glow emerges from him. It is heat and light and Spirit seeking form. It drifts into the air, searching.... searching for one who is worthy.

I raise my sword above my head and more power surges through me. Lightning flashes. Darkness blocks out the sun, turning day into night. Thunder crashes. Stars glow bright. And there, in the darkness, a beast takes form. A beast of midnight.

My dragon spreads its wings and blue fire erupts from its mouth.

Those who are still left alive and fighting look up and tremble. Fae and vampires drop their weapons and run. They scour to the winds. They scream to the heavens.

The Midnight Star has returned.

...

I am consumed by the power flowing through me, and it takes a moment to find myself again. Yami soars the dark skies, making sure everyone sees him, stopping the fighting by his mere presence.

It is Baron's cold wet nose pushing against my leg that pulls me back to the world. Fen! He's dying.

I run to him and drop to my knees. His body is burning up, his color is fading. I focus on the rune on my arm, and channel strength to lift Fen into my arms, carrying him all the way back to the castle despite the my own agonizing pain that is resurfacing now that my power is waning. I carry him through the retreating armies and soldiers collecting their dead. Through the fires. Through the chaos.

I find the closest room, a servant's quarters, grey and nearly empty, and place him on the bed. I need a healer, but I have no idea where to find one. "Baron, find Kal. Get him here immediately!"

Baron dashes out of the room, his paws leaving wet prints on the rug.

"Oh Fen. Wake up. Breathe. Live. I need you." I plead with him, my tears returning now that the rage has left me. Now I am only filled with heartache and fear. With a grief that threatens to undo me.

I rush to my room and fetch a bag with rudimentary healing supplies. When I return to Fen, I pull out a salve and rub it over his burned skin, where Oren's flaming blade touched him. I flinch, knowing how deep these burns go. Knowing that there is no salve that will heal this. He needs an ER with skin grafts and surgery. Not creams and herbs. I honestly don't know how he'll survive.

I need something stronger. Maybe in Kal's room...

I run into the hallway.

And into the tip of Levi's sword.

The Prince of Envy stares at me, rage in his eyes, fury in his voice. "You're one of them. The High Fae. The reason the Druids returned. The reason Ace nearly died. But once I kill you, they will slumber once more, and our kind will be safe."

"Levi, don't do this," I say. My voice wavers, my legs shake. "I need to get back to Fen. He's dying."

"Because of you! All of this, all of this blood and death... it's because of you."

I don't know what else to do, so I run. I run down the hall and turn the corner—

I crash into a man's arms. He holds me upright.

Levi turns the corner and halts, gazing past me.

I look up.

And see Ace.

He moves forward, putting his body between me and Levi, his brown cloak scraping the floor. He is pale, weak, and walks with a cane. Tools clang on his belt with every step.

"Brother, what is this?" he asks.

"Ace, let me through," Levi says. "She is High Fae. She deceived us. Just look at her hair, her ears. You know what must be done."

"And what of the contract?" Ace asks. "We are as bound by it as she is."

"You nearly died," Levi says. "I thought you would." His voice sounds broken now, small.

Ace puts his hand on Levi's arm. "But I didn't. I am here, alive. And I have come to see how my brothers fare, only to find you trying to kill the princess."

"It is the only way we will survive," Levi says.

"There are always other ways. Have I not taught you that in all these years?" Ace steps back, protecting me with his frail body. "I believe I will be claiming my month with the princess, brother. From now on, she is under my protection. If you wish to kill her..." Ace pauses, staring straight into his brother's eyes, "...you must kill me first."

EPILOGUE

Fenris Vane

"There are only flashes left. Only dust I try to grab in the wind. I remember... I remember a palace of white and gold. I remember spires that glow like the sun."

—Asher

Am I awake? Dreaming? Reality is suspended between time and space. I am there. In the nothingness that exists between darkness and light.

The pain is gone. I feel it as but a memory of what once was.

The air no longer smells of blood and metal, of battle and death. Of fire and brimstone.

The sky is blue and clear. The horizon glows with bright light. My body feels ethereal. There is a lightness to my being I have never known.

I walk forward in mist, but my feet do not find purchase on land. Am I floating? Am I dead?

I lost the battle. I left Arianna alone in a world torn by war. I failed her. I failed us. I failed my people. My kingdom.

There is a low growl to my right, and I look down, surprised to see Baron there. The white wolf seems one with the surroundings. I drop my hand to his head and wonder if he is real. Will my hand land on fur and flesh and bone, or will it fall through the illusion like smoke?

But he is there. I feel the heat of him, the silkiness of his fur, the presence of him. I choke up with emotion, and I cannot tell if I am grieving that my dearest friend has died with me, or if I am overcome with relief that I am not alone. Am I selfless or unforgivably selfish?

I am both.

I am neither.

I am nothing.

I keep walking. Floating. Moving forward into more mist and whiteness and otherness.

And then I hear her voice. She is humming a tune I did not know I knew. My soul responds to this music, this lullaby, with a visceral lurch that leaves me breathless.

She appears through the mist. Her wild white hair flies around her like a living thing, entwined with leaves and flowers, her dress falling at her bare feet, clinging to her body like roots and branches, seemingly made of the earth itself. Her eyes are large sapphires splashed against pale skin. She is a goddess. A woodland nymph.

And in my soul, I know who she is. "Mother," I whisper.

She is before me now, her hands reaching out for mine. When I grasp them they are warm, grounded in the earth.

"I have waited so very long to see you again," she says, her voice melodic, soft, full of the echoes of all that has ever been. "To hold you. To know you. But this isn't where you are meant to be."

"I am dead." It's such a strange thought, to be dead after being immortal for more generations than I can remember.

"You are neither dead, nor alive," she says. "You are being reborn."

"So I can go back?" My heart quickens at the thought. I need to go back, but the reasons are fading. The nothingness is stealing me away.

"If you wish," my mother says. "Do you wish it?"

"Arianna. I must go back for Arianna."

My mother smiles. "She needs you, and you need her. But you are more than you imagine yourself to be, my son. You are my heir. My legacy. I have given you everything."

Her words make no sense, and yet I know they are true. My mother died years ago, yes, but this was not her. This was not the woman in the images my brothers showed me. This was not the Queen who ruled hell with my father.

"I am the mother he hid from you," she says. "I am the mother of all. Once, I was a Keeper of nature, of life. And you are my heir."

The heir. The heir. The heir. The words just keep repeating themselves in my head. Baron nudges me, as if trying to communicate something of great import.

I wish he had words. I do not understand.

She reaches for me, hugs me close. I feel her power, it emanates from her, pouring into me, around me, alighting something new within. It burns. It chokes. It suffocates.

She pulls away. "Awake, my son. Live. Save your love. Save your people."

As she turns to walk away, her hair blows around in the wind. And I see.

I see.

I see.

Her ears.

She is Fae.

I am Fae.

...

It burns. It hurts. The air smells of death and blood and metal and war. My body is on fire. A rough tongue licks my face and I open my eyes to see Baron staring at me, his wolf face overcome with worry.

Something tears at my skin. Pain. I lean up on the bed and examine my body. A dark red cut covers my stomach. But it is fading. The dry blood falls away, and underneath, is new skin. Smooth and healthy. Something spreads there. A symbol, a tree, roots, branches. A tattoo.

Baron howls into the night. He grows luminous in the dark. Silver glyphs flash across his body, vanishing and appearing again. I do not understand what is happening, cannot recall where I am or why.

I gather my thoughts, and I remember. "Arianna!"

"She is gone from this place, brother." Asher sits on a chair in the dark, where I did not see him before. He leans forward, his cold face entering the light. "So, it is finally time. Time you learned who you are."

My breath is rapid and heavy, my body is slick with sweat. I do not know what he speaks of, but memories return to me. Memories of a dream. Of a woman.

I raise a hand to my ears...

And feel the pointed tips. "It can't be. I have memories. Memories of the land before."

Asher frowns. "Real memories? Or the ones you were told over and over?"

Real. They must have been. But I don't remember the story of my brothers in the Silver Gardens. I don't remember anything but flashes, images, places I had heard described over and over. Sometimes, I would struggle to recall the other world, but I would tell myself it had been thousands of years, my memory was fading. I had seen the same happen to my brothers. Was I never one of them? Was it all a lie?

Asher looks past me, his eyes faraway. "I remember the last battle, where the High Fae fell," he says softly. "We found a woman, dying amongst the corpses, and in her arms, a babe. She had given birth in the midst of battle, to a child born of war. But the babe was weak and near death. It made no sound. It barely breathed. And our mother, our mother took pity on the child. She gave it her blood and turned it into one of the Fallen. She said she would raise it as her own. And then the babe began to cry, and his Fae mother smiled, and passed from this world. Something left her body then. A Spirit on the wind. A white wolf. It licked the boy and vanished. Years later, when you found the wolf pup, I knew what it truly was. I knew the Spirit had taken form. And I knew you were its Keeper. You were the Earth Druid."

His eyes grow dark. His voice is soft. "So you see, brother, you were never one of us. You were always one of them."

TO BE CONTINUED

Call us Karpov Kinrade. We're the husband and wife team behind *Midnight Star*. And we want to say... Thank you for reading it. We worked hard on these characters and this world, and we're thrilled to share this story with so many readers. We hope you enjoyed *Midnight Star*, the second book in this fantasy series. Want to find out the moment the next book is available? Want to see a sneak peek of the next book cover and get teasers before launch? Sign up for the Karpov Kinrade/Vampire Girl newsletter and get all that and more at KarpovKinrade.com!

And visit our website for more great books to read. If you're looking for something to keep you engaged while you wait for the next *Vampire Girl* novel, check out *Court of Nightfall*. It's an epic adventure full of suspense, love, betrayal, friendship, and twists and turns that will leave you breathless. Keep reading for a look at *Court of Nightfall*, chapter 1.

USA TODAY BESTSELLING AUTHOR
KARPOV KINRADE

COURT OF
NIGHTFALL
NIGHTFALL CHRONICLES

PREFACE

Some say my story began when my parents were murdered. It did not.

Others say it began when I died. They are wrong.

I remember the pain.

The bullet of fire entered my body and moved through me, leaving a trail of burning agony in its wake.

I slumped over the crystal box that held the weapon we'd all fought to protect, my blood seeping out of me, staining the opaque quartz.

Red. Scarlet. Evie whispered the color of my own name into my ear as I slowly died.

My last vision was of that blood—still just grey to me—spreading into the cracks, into the intricate carvings that decorated the encasement. It almost seemed to glow, and I smiled and closed my eyes as the crystal shattered and darkness took me.

My story begins long before that—and if the historians take issue, I care not and neither should you. It's my story. I begin at the start.

With the test.

With the twins.

And what happened to them.

1

SHADES OF GREY

"Negative."

"Test me again."

The nurse shakes her head. "Sorry, Scarlett."

I slide off the table, rubbing under my shoulder where she took my blood. "The test is wrong."

She frowns. "Most kids would be grateful."

I walk to the door. "I'm not most kids."

The nurse escorts me to the waiting room, informs my parents of the results, and leaves. My parents sigh and exchange a look. My mom drops down to one knee and hugs me. "I know this isn't what you wanted, but—"

"The test is wrong," I say.

My dad stares at me for a moment. His voice is soft. "Why would you think that, Star?"

"I heal quick. I'm stronger than other girls my age." And I can just tell. It's my body. I can tell.

He bows his head.

My mom squeezes me tighter. "You're healthy. That doesn't make you Zenith."

They look tired, so I don't say any more. This day has been hard for everyone.

My mom sighs. "Why don't you go play outside while we fill out paperwork?"

I shrug and walk out the doors, passing posters of Zeniths stolen from their homes. A little girl with big eyes and a sad smile stares back at me from the eScreen in front of the office. She's out there somewhere. They all are. And it's no mystery who took them. It was Apex. He who runs the self-named group, The Apex, that traffics Zeniths for profit. But no one cares. So it will just keep happening. I understand why my parents are relieved. I just wish they understood why I'm not.

Kids squint at me from the playground, checking if I was tagged. When they don't see anything new on my ear they turn back to their play. One boy dives head first down the slide. It's red, with cracks in the thick plastic. I asked my dad the color once. I don't know what red looks like, but it's my favorite color. I turn away and run the dirt track around the school. Dust flies up around me. I build speed and jump, glancing at the gray sky, imagining I can fly. Not with an airplane, but with wings. I wish for them. But I don't tell anyone.

You don't dream of flying.

Not if you want to live.

...

There is war. You can hear it in the sobs of a mother weeping for her daughter. You can taste it in the rationed food and smell it on your tattered clothes. You can see it in the empty houses and roads and faces. You can feel it inside.

I'm a child, so people assume I know little of such things. But when you are young and free and happy, pain stands out all the more. I'm too little to fight, so I spend my days playing and planning. I plan to end the suffering.

"Why don't the Nephilim give up?" I ask, sitting on the swing, making patterns in the gravel with my foot. "They'll never conquer the world. It's a stupid plan."

"It's not about that," says Jax. He sits on the swing next to mine, his shirt dark and his pants darker. I can't see colors. I never have. But I imagine Jax is wearing blue. I hear it's a calm color. And I find Jax calming.

The sky is dark and cloudy. The rusty carousel we used to play on creaks in the wind. Two boys sit by a nearby anthill, poking at it with sticks as they laugh. So many of the children are gone.

Jax leans closer and lowers his voice. "One night, I heard my dad yelling at the eScreen. He said the Nephilim were fighting for their rights. He said all the news was a sham. I think he'd been drinking."

I cringe. My parents let me try wine last New Year's. The taste still disgusts me. But I noticed something about my parents that night. They answered all of my questions. "Sometimes, drunk people are more honest. Maybe your father's right. Maybe we should give the Nephilim rights."

He shakes his head, his hair falling in his eyes. "It's not so simple."

"No. But it can be." I finish a circle in the gravel. "One day, I'll leave the kingdom of Sky, and I'll train to be a Knight."

Jax sighs. "If we had the right families."

"I'll join a Domus first and work my way up the ranks, gain patronage, gain a patrician family. Then, I'll apply to be an Initiate. It's been done before."

Jax grins. "Then I'll join you. We'll be Jax the Courageous and Scarlett the Clever."

I giggle at my title. I only wish I understood my name better. Scarlett. I've tried to imagine the color, only to learn imagining a new color is impossible.

People tell me it's fiery and fierce.

I like that.

Jax looks over to the sand pit where a girl builds a castle. I've seen her around the playground and the park. We've spoken twice, both times about how to build proper fortifications. Her name's Brooke.

"Poor girl," says Jax, his eyes distant.

"What do you mean?" I ask. And then I see it.

The tag in her ear.

She tested Zenith.

The two boys notice the tag, too. The big one frowns and spits on the anthill. He nudges the small one, and they approach Brooke.

She doesn't notice them.

They kick her castle down.

"Hey!" she yells, standing, her hands balled in fists.

The big one shoves her back. "Get lost, Zenith scum," he says.

"Get lost, biter," says the small one.

They pick on her because she is different.

I've been different all my life. When people speak of colors, I speak of shades. It makes me no worse. They think this girl is weak and alone.

They are wrong.

I jump off my swing. I walk up behind them.

My parents tell me to approach things peacefully, but bullies aren't peaceful. They understand one thing. So I pick up a rock.

And throw it at the big one's head.

The collision with his skull is nearly silent. But the boy is not. He yells and collapses, grabbing at his bloody hair. His eyes are foggy.

The small one backs away.

The big one climbs to his knees. "Stupid Zenith lover. My big brother knows how to deal with you. He'll find you."

Jax walks up beside me. He's three years older and almost as big as the bully.

I palm another stone.

We say nothing.

The bullies exchange looks. Then the small one helps the big one up, and they walk away. "My brother will hear about you biters," yells the big one.

Fine. Let him tell others what I've done.

This world likes violence and winning.

And I'm good at both.

...

"Are you okay?" I ask.

The girl in front of us is tiny. My age, but shorter, more petite. She brushes a strand of hair off her face and shrugs. "Yeah. Thanks."

"Brooke! What happened?" Another girl runs up to us.

"Nothing. It's fine, Ella." Brooke turns to us. "I'm Brooke, this is my twin, Ella. Who are you?"

They look a lot alike, both dark haired with almond-shaped eyes and skin a few shades darker than my paleness, but where Brooke is unremarkable, someone who would blend into the crowd if not for how small she is, Ella would never blend in. She's got the face of a pixie, with big eyes and full lips and a dimple in her cheek. She's beautiful.

"I'm Scarlett. This is Jax."

We all awkwardly shake hands. They are both tagged. We aren't. If any of the teachers saw us they would separate us, but I don't care. I don't go to this school. I'm only here for the testing. They can take their segregation and discrimination and eat it.

"Do you want to play together?" I ask.

Brooke raises an eyebrow. "Really?"

Jax smiles. "Why not?"

We sit in the sand with them and begin building a castle. Brooke and Ella exchange a glance, then sit with us. Our hands dip into the cool sand and we pack it into shapes as our creation comes to life.

"Do you go to school here?" I ask, to break the silence.

Brooke nods. "Yes."

I smile. "We're homeschooled."

Brooke looks at up at us. "Are you brother and sister?"

I blush, but I don't know why. "No. But we might as well be."

"We've grown up together," Jax says with a grin. "I was there when Star was born."

We fall into silence after that, building our castle bigger and bigger. The twins occasionally exchange glances, and I wonder if they have a secret language like me and Jax. A way to communicate so others don't know.

I'm trying to add a tower to the castle when my sand collapses. "Again?"

Jax chuckles, tracing out a detailed window with a stick. "That's what happens when you don't plan out the foundation." We once competed in a wood carving competition. He built a palace with miniature knights. I built a house, though a lot of people mistook it for a rock.

Brooke grins and looks at Ella.

"Be careful," says Ella.

Brooke nods, then looks back at me. "Let me help."

She holds her hand over the castle, and the air buzzes. The sand comes together and floats. With care she moves her hand until the sand is packed into a tower.

"You're a Gravir," I say. "That's awesome."

Brooke smiles, but it slips from her face a moment later. "No one else would think so."

"They would, and they would be envious, and they would never admit it."

"Are you envious?" she asks.

I pause. "I try not to be."

Brooke bows her head, her eyes glistening.

I reach over and pat her hand. "There's nothing wrong with you. The problem is with them."

"How old are you?" Brooke asks me.

"I'm nine."

Brooke squints her eyes at me. "You don't sound like a normal nine-year-old."

Jax laughs. "She's not. I keep trying to figure out how she got so smart. I can only assume it's the great company she keeps." He nudges me playfully and I laugh with him, but inside I, too, wonder why I'm so different. I don't think like others, or respond like others my age, or even older. It's why I don't really have any friends other than Jax. The twins look at us strangely.

I don't know what more to say on the subject of my oddity, so I turn to Ella. "What can you do?" I ask, wanting to compliment her on her abilities as well.

Ella blinks a few times. "Notice my eyes?"

I squint. "What about them?"

Jax sighs. "Star's colorblind. She can't tell the difference."

"Oh," says Ella, playing with her hands sheepishly. "I can change the color of my eyes. I'm a dud."

I shake my head. "You may be listed as a dud in the system," I say, pointing to the building we came out of, "but that doesn't mean your abilities are useless. My mom is always trying to match her outfits to her eye color. You'll never have to worry about that."

After a moment, Ella smiles.

My parents emerge from the school, ready to go, but I ask if Jax and I can walk Brooke and Ella home instead. My mother glances at the tags on the girls' ears. "Where are your parents?" she asks.

"Home," says Brooke. "They knew we'd test positive."

My mom sighs, her lips in a tight line. My dad puts a hand on her shoulder. He looks at Jax and me. "Walk them home," he says.

We pass two people on the way. One sneers. The other takes one glance and imagines we don't exist. It takes five minutes to get to their house. On the porch, I ask if we can visit.

Ella turns stiff, but only for a second.

"Maybe," says Brooke. "I'll ask our mom. Thank you, for—"

There's a thud, like someone walking into a table, and a man in a loose tank top opens the door. His grey beard is uneven, and he smells like alcohol. He points at me with a beer bottle. "Who are you?"

"Scarlett. This is Jax."

"You bothering my kids?"

"No. We're friends."

He smirks like he doesn't believe me. "Brooke, Ella, come inside. You have chores to catch up on."

"Yes, Dad," says Brooke. The twins enter the house, and, with a swig of his beer, their dad slams the door shut in front of me. I sigh, hoping he treats his daughters with more manners than he treated me.

We walk down the porch, and I notice a mark below one of their windows. They must not have seen it yet, for they would have removed it. I clench my fists, wondering who painted the black A. Someone knows Zeniths live here.

Someone wants them gone.

...

On the way home, we pass a gated community, a Zenith-Free sign on the door. Old posters of a Knight in silver armor cover the light posts. The text underneath reads: *Zenith? Then we want you. Fight for the Orders.* A figure cloaked in black with a mask of white is spray painted on a wall. The words *Nox Aeterna* are written next to him in thick spiky text. The graffiti is of Nyx, leader of the Nephilim, the one they consider a saint, maybe even a god. The boy who painted it was captured and executed two days ago. I saw it on the news.

I stop and stare at the painting, surprised no one has removed it yet.

Jax looks at me. "I know what you're thinking," he says with a frown.

"What am I thinking?" I ask with a challenge in my voice.

"Dangerous thoughts."

"It's not dangerous to dream," I tell him.

"When those dreams involve flying with Nephilim it is."

I've never told Jax about my secret dreams to fly with the Nephilim, but he knows me too well. He always has. I scowl at him. "You don't know anything about it, Jaxton Lux."

He grins and nudges me. "You can't hide yourself from me, Scarlett Night. I see you."

I ignore him and keep walking. He just chuckles and catches up with me in long strides.

We pass the small church. The grass around it is dead. I attend, but only when it's mandatory. I respect the religion, the values, but the priest preaches more. He speaks of Fallen Angels and how they had children with man. How those children, Nephilim, are our enemy. And how if you are Zenith, then your ancestors bred with Nephilim, and your bloodline has sinned, and you are sinful, and you must repent every day of your life.

I do not believe people should be held accountable for the mistakes of others. Even if the Angels who fell were cruel and deadly, why does it make all their children so?

Every year, the priest reminds us that we used to be three estates: plebeian, patrician, and clergy. It was only plebeians, like me, who chose to mate with Angels. They created the sinful Zeniths. And now, we are four estates. It is why patricians rule, he says. Because they remained pure.

I focus back on the present as Jax and I turn the corner. A Streetbot, which looks like a large ball on wheels, hums and beeps irregularly. The robot strikes the curb over and over, stuck until its battery dies. Years ago, a maintenance crew would have fixed the issue in a few hours. Now, no one will come. I grab the Streetbot and turn it around, and it rolls down the road, on track once again.

Jax stands beside me, staring ahead. "It won't get any cleaning done. Its dusters are jammed. "

"I know. It just seemed wrong to leave it that way."

"What way?"

"Stuck in a life it wasn't meant for," I say softly.

He nods, and we watch the robot disappear into the sunset.

...

We arrive at a sprawling farmhouse with a chipped roof. Faded paint peels in the corners and the front porch creaks, but it's home, it's where I was born, and it fills me with a kind of peace.

A small tree grows in our front yard, shifting in the wind. I pat the dirt— freshly watered—and check the strength of its branches. They're strong.

My dad and I planted the tree a few months ago. He let me pick, and I picked a weeping willow. They remind me of the maidens in old tales.

It grows darker, and Jax and I walk inside. My mom and dad sit together on the couch, watching the eScreen. There is an image of a man in shackles. There is a crowd around him, throwing stones and food. They scream for blood. The man—

The eScreen turns black.

My dad holds the remote. He smiles. "How was the walk?"

"Long," I say. "What are you watching?"

"Boring grown-up stuff. You know how we are." He chuckles and stands. "Hey, how about you and I go flying?"

I know this a distraction, but it's a good one. I nod.

Jax faces my mom. "Anything I can help with?" he asks.

"There are some dishes left."

Without hesitation, he marches into the kitchen. I hear the tap water start. Jax always helps around the house, and he stays here most nights. His father doesn't seem to mind. He and Jax don't get along.

I follow my dad outside, to the small runway behind our house. He hands me a clipboard with the preflight checklist. "Want to help me out?"

I take it from him and focus on checking the engines and gas. My palm flattens against the cool steel of the plane and I close my eyes, imagining the flight, the feeling of weightlessness as the air currents propel me into the endless sky.

I work in a daze, and when I'm done, a large hand lands on my shoulder—strong, warm, comforting. I look up at my dad.

"Ready?"

I climb in next to him, my heart beating harder in my chest as my body prepares to surrender to the shift in gravity. My dad turns on the engine, and the seat rumbles beneath me. We drive down the strip.

And become airborne.

My stomach drops and my heart stammers. But as we drift higher, amongst the clouds, my breathing slows. Here, up in the sky, I am at ease.

I grin out the window and try to imagine what a blue horizon would look like. Though the sun is setting now.

There would be reds and oranges then. Not blue. It's hard to remember how things change in colors. For me it's only shifting shades of grey.

I watch our house fade into the distance. "When I grow up," I say. "I'm going to be the best pilot the world has ever seen."

My dad glances over at me, his smile briefly wilting. "You have lots of time to figure that stuff out, Star. No need to rush."

He doesn't understand, but he will someday. I know the course of my life. And nothing will change me.

...

That night, while Jax watches movies in the basement, my parents sit me down, and my mom hands me a cup of hot chocolate. It's her way of asking forgiveness for what's about to happen.

"What's wrong?" I ask.

My parents share a look and a frown.

"Nothing," my dad says. "Everything is fine. But we wanted to talk to you about your future."

I relax into the kitchen chair and smile. We've had similar talks before. They said I shouldn't go into a Teutonic Domus with my heart set on being a pilot. I said I'd consider their opinion.

They exchange that parental glance that's endearing and annoying at the same time. Their wordless communications that I envy.

My mom presses her lips together in a line. "So you want to be a pilot?"

I nod and sip the hot drink. "That's the plan."

"Star, there are requirements for getting into that program. For even getting a pilot's license. Physical requirements."

I look between them, confused. "I'm healthy. Strong. And when I'm older—"

"There's a vision test," my dad says.

My heart flutters in my chest. "I can see just fine."

"Star—"

"My vision is 20/20. Better, even."

"Star—"

"It doesn't matter that I can't see color."

My mom sighs and takes my hand. I know what she wants to say, and I don't want to hear it. She must know it, too, because she smiles. "Maybe they'll change the rules by the time you're older. But... " she raise a finger before I can interrupt, "But... you should have another plan."

I swallow the rock in my throat. I don't show emotion in my voice. "I'll consider your opinion."

They nod.

I leave my half-finished hot chocolate on the table. Then I stand and run upstairs and slam my door. I fall into my bed and weep.

...

My parents think they can control my path. They are wrong.

I grab my laptop. The airplane sticker on the cover is half torn. I tear off what remains. Then I search for the video my parents wouldn't let me see. It's not available publicly online yet, but that's not a problem. My mom got me hooked on computers as a kid. When I could barely walk, I was already learning to type. A year ago Jax declared me the world's best hacker.

I find the video and play it. A man, handcuffed, is escorted down a street by another man dressed in long robes. People gather around, gawking.

I hear someone twist the handle on my door, and I click the power button to shut down the video before they come in.

"What were you just watching?" my mom asks.

I shrug, playing it cool. "Just something I found online. It's—"

She sits down next to me on my bed. "Scarlett? Are you lying right now?"

I debate whether to keep lying, but my mom would know. She always knows. "Yes," I say, shoulders slumping.

She smiles gently. "Then let's try again. What were you just watching?"

"The news reel you wouldn't let me see. I hacked the news network."

I glance up at her to gauge her level of mad, but she's suppressing a grin. "Why?"

"Because you wouldn't let me watch it. Zeniths are being mistreated, and people need to do something. *I* need to do something."

"What do you intend to do?" she asks, still curious more than anything.

I think about it, glad I'm not in trouble—yet. "Well, I haven't settled on a plan. With some time, I could hack the Inquisition security system."

She shifts on the bed to look at me better. "If you do, they will find you."

"I could cover my tracks."

She tilts her head, a long curl coming undone from her clip and falling over her shoulder. "Some of them. But, Star, understand that other people have been at this for far longer than you. Whatever you can do right now, no matter how amazing, Inquisition security can do much better."

I fold my arms across my chest, knowing I probably look like a pouty kid but not caring. "But I have to do something."

She smiles again, her eyes crinkling. "You can keep practicing."

"Practicing doesn't change anything," I say, dropping my chin to my chest as feelings of impotence and frustration build in me.

My mom is still for a moment, her eyes distant, reflective, before she focuses on me again. "Come with me," she says. "I want to show you something." She stands and leaves the room, walking downstairs.

I hurry to follow. "What?"

"The video I didn't let you watch," she says over her shoulder.

The eScreen in our living room covers nearly the entire wall in a grey reflective material. With it we can access networks or play videos sent via satellite signal from an eGlass. My parents both own one. I have one on my Christmas list.

My mom clicks her eGlass and a video appears. A man is tied to a beam on a wooden platform surrounded by hay. People circle him, throwing food, stones, rotten vegetables, calling him names and sneering.

Another man dressed in a cloak walks forward holding a torch, speaking to the crowd, but the people are too loud to hear the Inquisitor's words.

"That man on trial was a hacker," my mom says. "He wiped multiple Inquisition bank accounts. They found him a day later."

I feel a small surge of pride for what he did. "He must have really messed them up."

My mom sits on the couch, and I join her as she asks, "Do you think those accounts mattered?"

"I imagine they would. Money's important, right? But... " I think about it more and realize... "The Inquisition isn't hurting for money, are they? They can always get more."

My mom nods.

"Well," I say, "at least he showed people they could fight back."

"Did he?" my mom asks. "Or did he simply become another example of the Inquisition's power?"

I look back up at the video just as the Inquisitor sets the torch to the haystack. As the hacker begins to burn, his cries mixing with the cheers of the crowd, my mom shuts off the video and sets the display to a serene mountain scene.

She turns to me and reaches for my hand, squeezing. "My Star, one day, when you're older, you'll make a difference. A *real* difference. But you need to be ready. Hone your skills. And..." she ruffles my hair, "try to avoid stupid mistakes." She stands and walks toward the kitchen, and I slump in the couch, depressed.

All of my practicing was for nothing. I don't want to end up like that guy in the video. "I guess I'll stop hacking then," I announce to the world in all my despondent pre-teen angst.

My mom turns back, a mischievous grin forming on her face. "I didn't say to stop," she says, winking. "I just said to be careful."

ABOUT THE AUTHOR

Karpov Kinrade is the pen name for the husband and wife writing duo of USA TODAY bestselling, award-winning authors Lux Kinrade and Dmytry Karpov.

Together, they write fantasy and science fiction.

Look for more from Karpov Kinrade in *Vampire Girl*, *The Nightfall Chronicles*, *The Forbidden Trilogy* and *The Shattered Islands*.

They live with three little girls who think they're ninja princesses with super powers and who are also showing a propensity for telling tall tales and using the written word to weave stories of wonder and magic.

Find them at www.KarpovKinrade.com

On Twitter @KarpovKinrade

On Facebook /KarpovKinrade

And subscribe to their newsletter for special deals and up-to-date notice of new launches. www.ReadKK.com.

~~~~~

If you enjoyed this book, consider supporting the author by leaving a review wherever you purchased this book. Thank you.

Made in the USA
Middletown, DE
16 July 2018